CONCEALED IN SHADOW

A CASSIE QUINN MYSTERY

L.T. RYAN

with

K.M. ROUGHT

LIQUID MIND MEDIA

THE CASSIE QUINN SERIES

Path of Bones

Whisper of Bones

Symphony of Bones

Etched in Shadow

Concealed in Shadow

Betrayed in Shadow

1

JOSEPH ARTHUR ZBIRAK DID NOT CONSIDER HIMSELF A PICKY EATER. HE did, however, take his steak seriously. He needed it well-seasoned and medium rare. Warm and pink in the middle. Delectable and juicy. Anything less than a perfect cut would not enter his mouth under any circumstances.

With an apologetic smile and a soft voice, he sent his steak back to the kitchen. Medium *rare*, he had said, hoping the young waitress would relay the message to the cook. The bubbly girl wore her dark hair in a ponytail and a smattering of enamel pins on her waist apron. Zbirak would give her a hearty tip, regardless of the mistake. It wasn't her fault, after all.

Around a mouthful of food, the man sitting across from Zbirak said, "Hope you don't think I'm gonna wait for you." He was rotund and ruddy-faced, topped off with a bad comb-over. His mustache was untrimmed, and years of sweat stained the armpits of his shirt. The man talked as he chewed, spraying as much as he swallowed. "I never knew you had such delicate sensibilities."

Zbirak wanted to glower, but he refrained from taking the bait. Other than sharing the same first name, he and Pisano had nothing in common. Where the other man was fat, rude, and incapable of thinking for himself, Zbirak was lean, quiet, and clever. Genetics had blessed him with an average face and enough brains to know when to act and when to sit back and bide his time.

Pisano, on the other hand, was all bluff. It had carried him through forty-two years on the police force, not unscathed. In his youth, his fists sealed the deal when his words failed to do their job. Now it was merely arrogance. For someone who couldn't throw or take a punch without wheezing, he sure was a cocky son of a bitch.

"I like what I like." Zbirak shrugged, a playful smile tugging at the corners of his mouth. He wouldn't let this man get under his skin. "And when I make a request, I expect it to be fulfilled."

For the first time, Pisano revealed the disquiet Zbirak instilled in him. "Look, it wasn't my fault." Shoving the rest of his burger into his mouth, he licked a bit of mustard from his pinky finger. After draining his beer, he dove into his fries, shoving them into his mouth three at a time. He didn't even make fleeting eye contact. "But I'm taking care of it."

"Oh?" Zbirak raised an eyebrow. The return of the server held his inquiry at bay. She set his new plate in front of him. "Thank you."

"Please let me know if that's to your liking, sir."

Zbirak took his fork in one hand and his knife in the other, cutting the steak against the grain to reveal a pink center. Juice poured from the opening and pooled beneath the meat, threatening to mix with the heap of mashed potatoes sitting to one side. Looking up at the server, he smiled with all his teeth. "It's perfect. Please thank the chef for me."

"Of course." The woman flicked her ponytail over her shoulder to get it out of the way. "Is there anything else I can do for you, gentlemen?"

"That'll be all, for now." Zbirak kept his smile steady and noticed the way it mesmerized her. "My friend and I have some business to attend to. Would it be all right if you gave us some privacy until we're ready for the check?"

"Absolutely." The woman backed away. "Flag me down if you need anything else."

Zbirak watched as she retreated before returning to his steak and cutting a healthy portion from one end. It was what he had been craving all day. His mouth watered as he sunk his teeth into that glorious first bite. The restaurant was three stars at best—rustic in an upscale sort of way—but they had a solid menu. Most people would've been happy with the cut they'd received, but Zbirak was nothing if not a perfectionist.

"You got an unhealthy relationship with your meat, pal." Pisano's rough voice cut through Zbirak's moment like a knife through flesh. "Let me know if you need a minute alone."

Zbirak scoffed. Between the two of them, he wasn't the unhealthy one. But Pisano's barbs were blunt and not worth Zbirak's time. "Tell me exactly how the problem is being taken care of."

"All right, all right. Keep your pants on." Pisano wiped his hands on a napkin and threw it back onto the table. He looked Zbirak in the eye for the first time in several minutes. Ah, there was some of his renowned bluster. The man who had failed one too many times took more offense to being called out for his shortcomings than one confident that he would not disappoint you again. "Would I lie to you?" He guffawed, and it turned several heads. "I'm stupid, but I'm not that stupid."

"Yes, you would." Zbirak took another bite, but he found he couldn't enjoy his meal under these conditions. Placing his knife and fork on the table, he said. "And yes, you are."

"I don't like your tone."

This time, Zbirak laughed. A quiet chuckle that no one but Pisano heard. Often, he found humor in men who knew better than to test him, but did so anyway because their pride meant more to them than their life. Zbirak leaned forward, though he didn't relish being any closer to Pisano than necessary. "I gave you a job. You failed."

"A momentary setback is not a failure." Even Pisano seemed surprised by his rather insightful retort. "She slipped away for now, but we'll get her back. Just wait and see."

"And how, exactly, did she slip away?"

Pisano must've gotten the sense that Zbirak already had the

answer because he didn't bother lying. "I sent my nephew to grab her, and she ran. Simple as that."

"I was very specific in my instructions that you be the one to pick her up. Not your nephew."

"I had a prior engagement. Look." Pisano shifted in his seat. Placing a hand on his side, he winced. When he spoke again, there was a strain in his voice. "I didn't think some random woman would be that hard to nab. No way she knew we were after her."

"Gender has nothing to do with survival instincts." Zbirak leaned back in his chair, no longer able to maintain his proximity to Pisano's form. "Society has trained women to distrust everyone, especially a dim-witted thug such as your nephew. Your police uniform, however, would have lured her into a false sense of security."

"I figured she'd get spooked if she saw an Atlanta cop knocking on her door in Savannah."

"There you go, thinking for yourself again." Zbirak kept himself from sneering, but only just. "She would've trusted you because she thinks all the Savannah cops are crooked."

"She's not wrong." Pisano burped, but it didn't appear to relieve any of the pain in his side. Sweat had accumulated along his brow. "I said I'll take care of it." He peered over his shoulder. "They got a bathroom in this place?"

"There's no need. I did it myself."

Pisano turned back to him. "The woman? You found her?"

"No, your nephew." Zbirak pushed his plate away. The smell emanating from the sweaty man across the table had ruined his appetite. What a shame. "I took care of him."

Pisano groaned, but Zbirak couldn't decide if it was agony over losing his nephew or the agony in his gut. "My sister is going to kill me."

"I assure you she is not." Zbirak wiped his mouth with a cloth napkin and tossed it on the table next to his plate. Standing, he wrapped one of his large hands around Pisano's fleshy arm, trying not to recoil at the dampness of the man's shirt. "Come on, I'll help you to the bathroom."

"How do you know?" Pisano was sweating profusely. Every word sounded like a struggle.

Zbirak didn't answer right away. First, he led Pisano into the men's room and directed him to the last stall. It was wheelchair accessible, which allowed both of them to fit comfortably at once. Pisano collapsed to the floor and crawled on his hands and knees until he slumped over the toilet, his nose almost touching the water in the bowl. Zbirak closed the door behind them.

"I know your sister will not kill you because I already have."

Pisano lifted his head enough to look at Zbirak, but the light in his eyes was fading. "Wh-what? Wh-why?"

"As I said," Zbirak responded, taking a step closer to the man. He didn't want Pisano to misinterpret his words, even with death looming overhead. "When I make a request, I expect it to be fulfilled."

"I'll find her," Pisano blustered. "I-I'll do it. Please." He coughed, and blood-laced spittle ran down his chin. "Help me."

"You're far beyond help." Zbirak tried not to revel in this man's undoing, but it was difficult. It was not the first time he had considered killing Pisano. "I had a simple request, Joseph. Kill Mrs. Sherman. I sent you because you are a cop. Instead, you employed your nephew with as much tact and brains as you have and no badge to back it up. He scared her away, and now she's in the wind. I will find her eventually, but I will waste valuable time and resources to do so."

"I-I'm s-sorry." Pisano's breaths were wet and gasping. Red blooms filled the toilet water, having dripped from his mouth and nose. "P-please—"

"Don't beg." Zbirak didn't hide his disdain now. "You should've known better, Joseph. The only thing I hate more than having my time wasted is a loose end. Mrs. Sherman is a loose end that my employer expects me to trim. I entrusted that job to you, and you failed. I killed your nephew because you gave him information that was not yours to share. I killed you because you have been a pain in my ass for two decades, and my patience has run thin."

Pisano was purple in the face. Mouth opening and closing like a fish gasping for oxygen, but the sound of air moving through his lungs was absent. The man only had a few moments left, and he would spend them in excruciating pain. It was a blessing, all things considered. If Zbirak had more time, he would've dragged out Pisano's death for days.

"You're a disgusting, arrogant bastard who only made it this far in life because of the handouts you received along the way." Zbirak wanted to spit on him but resisted. "If you had a modicum of self-awareness, you would've come here begging for your life instead of maintaining your mask of false bravado. Perhaps I may have even considered sparing you."

Pisano's body had gone still, and the smell emanating from his pants indicated he could no longer hear Zbirak's words. It would take a few hours before anyone realized there was a dead body in the stall, and that would be more than enough time for Zbirak to put distance between himself and the restaurant.

As he exited the restroom and returned to his seat, Zbirak motioned for the server. "My friend is ill." He rearranged his face into a frown. "Which means I'll take this time to pay the bill."

"Oh no." She glanced down at Pisano's empty plate. "Do you think—"

"Doubtful." Zbirak transformed his frown into another brilliant smile. "He's got a sensitive stomach. I keep telling him he'll eat himself into an early grave."

Following his cue, she laughed at the joke, then pointed to his plate. "Would you like a box for your steak?"

Zbirak couldn't stomach the idea of trying to reheat his meal without overcooking it. He'd rather see it go to waste. "Just the check, please."

The woman took their plates, but when she reached for Pisano's beer bottle, Zbirak's hand shot out to stop her. He wrapped his fingers around the neck and smiled up at her. "This can stay." If the woman thought his actions were strange, her face didn't betray her. Bounding away, she returned a few moments later with the check. Waiting for her to retreat once more, he dropped a wad of cash on the table, slid the beer bottle into the pocket of his jacket, and strode out the front door.

Once the staff realized Pisano was still in the bathroom, they would send a busboy in to check on him. When the kid discovered the dead body, they would call the Atlanta PD, who would question Zbirak's server. She'd describe the man at the table as white, with brown hair and a kind smile. He had an average build with no distinguishing features, likely in his forties. By then, the kitchen staff would have washed away any evidence of fingerprints from their leftover food. He'd wiped off the lock on the stall and the handle on the door before exiting the bathroom. Not to mention he'd tossed the beer bottle in a dumpster three miles across town. Any traces of the poison he'd poured into its open mouth while Pisano was distracted would disappear in a matter of days.

And just like that, Zbirak would slip back into the shadows like he had the past twenty-five years. His spirits were soaring as he merged onto the highway half an hour later, certain no one had followed him. His only regret was that he'd let Pisano ruin his dinner.

No matter. Once Mrs. Sherman was out of the picture, he'd sit down for another steak dinner. And this time, he wouldn't make the mistake of inviting anyone else to the table.

2

THE CHICAGO HISTORICAL SOCIETY WAS FOUNDED IN 1856 TO STUDY and interpret the city's storied past. After pieces of their collection succumbed to fire—twice—the CHS moved their museum and library to Lincoln Park, boasting over twenty-two million items exploring the city's influence on American history. With the city backdrop to the West and Lake Michigan to the East, the Chicago History Museum collects snapshots of time and preserves them for all to witness.

One of the great ironies of Cassie Quinn's life was that she loved museums. The smell, the atmosphere, the people, the history, the influence—all of it. You could walk into a museum and transport yourself to Ancient Egypt, where a toilet was merely a hole in a stool, then fast forward to a time in which a man named Marcel Duchamp could place a urinal upside down in a gallery and call it a fountain. Nowhere else in the world could you find such a strange amalgamation of historically and intellectually significant objects. It placed the breadth of human achievement under a single roof.

But Cassie could not celebrate museums without also acknowledging the elephant in the room. Lord Elgin famously stole pieces of the Parthenon and transported them to Britain, where they continue to reside in the British Museum. Vandalism and theft were not solitary events, and many European museums have refused to return the legacies of other countries to their rightful places. If Greece cannot retrieve their beloved history, imagine the likelihood that an African nation could convince England to give up their cultural property, nearly all of which dwells outside of the continent.

Even the Chicago History Museum has an uncomfortable past to atone for. Lincoln Park was once a municipal burial ground for over thirty-five thousand people, many of whom had died of cholera. But the earth at the edge of the lake was loose and sandy, and they had buried the bodies below the water table, risking contamination of the city's water supply.

In the mid to late-1800s, the bodies were transferred from the park to rural cemeteries outside the city limits. Not all could be located. The Great Chicago Fire of 1871 destroyed many of the markers, and estimates indicated ten thousand bodies could still be buried beneath the soil of the park. Every time someone brought in a backhoe—like during one of the Chicago History Museum's several expansions—more bones would surface.

And there was the irony—Museums tested Cassie's mental fortitude like no other place on the planet. When she crossed the threshold into a cemetery, she knew what she was getting into. There was bound to be a ghost who approached her, begging for help. But in a museum, there were no rules. Ghosts and visions assaulted her senses. Millions of objects harbored information from the past, waiting for the right person to walk by. Pair that with tens of thousands of spirits who had passed through the grounds, and it was hard to say whether Cassie could truly have a good time within the confines of such a place.

But something had shifted in that trip to New Orleans. Sabine Delacroix had turned a key and unlocked Cassie's powers. Her abilities were nowhere near stable or perfect, but for the first time in her life, she was confident. She had patience. She trusted the answers would come in due time. New Orleans had opened her eyes to infinite possibilities. She didn't want to run and hide anymore. She wanted to help those forgotten by the annals of time. With a newfound purpose, Cassie walked a little taller.

Nevertheless, exploring the Chicago History Museum was no easy feat. She could feel the artifacts tugging on her consciousness, begging to be heard. Spirits drifted by, untethered yet imprisoned within a world where they had been relegated to myth and legend. The older the ghost, the further gone. But the younger ones were still hungry for answers, and they often went to great lengths to seek her out.

Cassie already had a mission, and the museum was merely a pit stop along the way—somewhere to let the morning hours tick by while she awaited Harris's arrival. She wandered aimlessly, allowing the current of the universe to determine her destination, until she stopped in front of one of the most prominent oil-on-canvas paintings in the building. *Memories of the Chicago Fire in 1871*, painted from memory forty-one years later by Julia Lemos, who had witnessed the historical event firsthand.

Billowing clouds of smoke stretched across the sky as tendrils of flame consumed buildings from the inside out, like a parasite, with no concern for the longevity of its host. Its fuel was too willing to accept its embrace, and so the fire feasted like a king.

Dozens of people fled the scene, their dark clothes in contrast to the pollution overhead. Cassie could hear the calamitous event like she had a crackling speaker up to her ear. People shouting, horses neighing, and wood crackling as the blaze consumed the city without pause or prejudice.

She had been to Chicago once in her youth and vowed never to return. As a teenager, she had buried her abilities so deep within herself that they were nearly non-existent. *Nearly.* The city had always given her a headache and caused her stomach to twist in response to an unseen force. While the migraines were a distant memory, the knot in her abdomen curled in on itself until Cassie winced. She had to loosen her muscles and tell her body to relax. But it was difficult to convince herself she wasn't in any immediate danger when she could feel the inferno's heat caressing the back of her neck.

A vibration in her pocket broke Cassie from her daze, and a smile spread across her face when she saw Jason's name light up her phone. Her skin cooled, the knot loosened further, and the sound of screaming men, women, and children faded away to a dull roar that she tucked into the deepest recesses of her mind.

"Hey." Cassie's voice was breathless with surprise. Even from a thousand miles away, he had that effect on her. "Miss me already?"

"Can you blame me?" There was a chuckle in Jason's voice that made her heart skip a beat. Even if he was playing into her joke, it was nice to hear. "How was your flight? Did you make some more friends?"

Cassie's laugh echoed around the hall. A few heads turned, and she winced in response. Stepping back from the painting, she nestled into a corner where she wouldn't disturb anyone else. "Yeah, I met a time-traveling wizard. Nice guy. Terrible fashion sense."

Jason laughed, but the humor didn't linger.

"What's wrong?" she asked. Her first thought was the pets. "Is Apollo okay? Bear?"

"They're fine, I promise. They might even miss you as much as I do." The words brought a smile to Cassie's face, but it didn't last long. "Jane Livingston asked Magdalena if you're still interested in your job."

Cassie froze. "What? Why?"

"You've been missing a lot of work."

"They've approved all my time off."

"I know." Jason sighed, and the air from his mouth made the phone crackle in her ear. "That's why Jane hasn't said anything to you. But if she's asking Mags whether you're still interested, then they're probably wondering if all this time off is becoming a pattern." There was a deadening silence on the phone before Jason blew out another breath of air. "I'm sorry, I feel like I'm being the bad guy here."

"You're not. I know you're not." She tapped her foot on the ground until someone looked at her pointedly. Putting her back to them, she lowered her voice. "Has Jane said anything to you yet?"

"No, but I'm not sure if she's aware of our... relationship."

Cassie's heart fluttered at the word. The last time she'd seen Jason, they'd shared a kiss outside her hotel room. They hadn't talked about labels or exclusivity, and Cassie was afraid if she broached the topic, she'd jinx the whole thing. "I'm choosing not to worry about it for now," she declared. "They approved my time off, so there's nothing they can say about it. When I get home, I'll work overtime to make sure I wrap up all my projects. And then some."

"Do you know when you're coming back yet?"

"No idea. I'm supposed to meet Adelaide in a few minutes. Once I talk with her, I'll have a better idea of what's going on." She wasn't used to sharing her fears with people, so she had to force out the next words. "I'm worried about her."

"How come?"

"She's not acting like herself." Cassie sagged into the wall. All she wanted to do was crawl back into bed. "She won't leave Chicago without answers."

"I know she's important to you," Jason started, "and not just because she was also important to David." He hesitated, like he was measuring each word to make sure it held exactly the right weight. "But don't let her drag you into something you're not ready for, okay? It's hard enough losing someone, but it's a whole different ballgame when you have to investigate their death, too. Trust me, I know."

Jason hadn't shared his story with Cassie yet, but this wasn't the first time he'd mentioned he knew how she was feeling. Even without all the details, the idea comforted her—momentarily, at least. Then she'd remember how David had written her a letter specifically telling her not to investigate his murder, and she'd felt the guilt swell up inside her again. "Thank you." A comforting silence filled the phone. It was nice just to exist together. "You probably have to go soon."

"Keep me updated, okay?" There was a strain to his voice. "And be careful."

"I will," she said, though it wasn't really a promise she could make. "I'll text you once we know anything new."

After Cassie hung up, she took a moment to breathe. Somewhere over the course of the conversation, her anxiety had ratcheted up, threatening to constrict her throat and lungs against her will. The heat of the museum didn't help matters, and with great abandon, she wound her way back toward the entrance and picked up her duffel bag at the luggage storage area. She hadn't gone home before heading to Chicago, so she was wearing all the clothes she'd had in New Orleans. In other words, she wasn't prepared for winter in Chicago, and had stopped to buy a heavy winter coat she'd never use back home. But it'd be worth it to ensure she didn't lose any limbs to frostbite.

Stepping outside, she relished how the cold pierced her skin and shocked her body into forgetting about the burden she carried. Turning left, Cassie strolled down the street toward a tiered fountain at the end of the road. Hooking left again, she meandered along a path lined with bare trees. The city had seen its first snow a month ago, and the frozen ground made sure it couldn't melt away. The end of December was approaching, and unlike Savannah, Chicago rarely went without a white Christmas.

As Cassie neared a crossroads, a figure rounded the corner and stopped in the middle of the path. Even from a distance, Cassie recognized Harris's telltale silhouette, complete with a slicked-back ponytail and a pair of aviators. A long wool coat covered most of her outfit, but Cassie could tell Harris had given up her pantsuit for a pair of jeans. The Timberlands on her feet were in stark contrast to the glossy sheen of the pavement.

Cassie looked past Harris and out across the expanse of Lincoln Park. She felt the spirits more than she saw them, and she wondered how she could navigate a city so full of tragedy without being pulled under the waves. At one time, she would've been happy to lean on Harris for support, but these days, Cassie couldn't trust the detective wouldn't risk her drowning just to get a few answers.

It was too late to turn back now, and when Harris raised her hand in greeting, Cassie returned the gesture, plastering a smile on her face and praying to God that the Windy City wouldn't blow them off course.

3

Cassie waited until she was within earshot of Harris. "Hey, how are you?"

Harris pursed her mouth. "Don't say it like that."

"Like what?"

"Like you're *worried* about me."

"What's wrong with being worried about you?"

"How would you feel if I asked you like that?" Harris placed a hand on Cassie's shoulder and stared straight into her eyes. *"How are you?"*

"I would be grateful."

"You'd be offended."

"Fine." Cassie rolled her eyes. "I'll pretend like I don't care."

"You're not supposed to worry about me," Harris amended. "I'm supposed to worry about *you*."

"Okay, now I *am* offended."

A smile broke across her face. "Good."

"Seriously, though." Cassie didn't want to press the subject, but they couldn't avoid it forever. "After you dragging me to Chicago on a whim, I'm allowed to check in."

"It wasn't a whim, and I didn't drag you here," Harris said. "And yes, I'm fine. All things considered."

All things considered. Cassie let the phrase roll around her head. It tasted bitter. The *thing* they were considering was David's death. Putting her best friend's murder aside, she'd say she was fine, too. But how could she not think about him? He took up every inch of her brain space. She couldn't get away from it if she tried. And she'd tried.

"Whim or no whim," Cassie said, "I can't stay here long. People are asking questions at work and I can't miss many more days."

Harris's playful air vanished. "We're talking about figuring out what happened to David. *David*," she said, as if Cassie had forgotten. "Let them ask questions."

"I can't lose my job, Adelaide."

Harris took a big breath and held it for a few seconds before exhaling through her mouth. "I know. I'm sorry." She looked like she meant it, but frustration still coated her words. "Believe me, I appreciate you coming out here with me. The dead of winter isn't the best time to be in Chicago."

As if on cue, an icy breeze tore through the park. Cassie pulled her jacket up around her neck. "I miss Savannah."

Harris spread her arms wide. "Don't get me wrong, I love Chicago. It reminds me of Montana." She cut a glance sideways. "But I can't deny that in Georgia you're less likely to lose a couple appendages to frostbite."

"Let's walk." Cassie gestured to the path ahead and hiked her bag up higher on her shoulder. "I can already feel the hypothermia setting in."

"Don't be such a baby," Harris replied. Cutting to the left, she led Cassie down another path.

Cassie pushed her hands deep into her pockets. "Tell me more about this flash drive."

"I haven't looked through the whole thing yet—"

Cassie stopped dead in her tracks. "Wait. You see one piece of information that points to Chicago, and you decide to hop on a plane before going through the entire thing?"

Harris rolled her eyes and grabbed the crook of Cassie's elbow, dragging her forward. "Relax. I've gone through most of it, but there's still a lot to figure out. Some of it's coded. Some of it's a bunch of numbers without context. These things take time."

The chill in the air made Cassie snippy. "And remind me again why we're here?"

With all the patience of a parent explaining to her child why the sky is blue, Harris said, "Randall Sherman was an accountant. A few weeks ago, he came forward to turn on Aguilar. We figured he was running Aguilar's books." She patted the pocket of her wool coat. "And considering what's on this drive, it looks like we were right."

"Why did he turn on Aguilar?"

"His wife is pregnant. He thought he was in too deep, and he got cold feet."

Cassie felt like a broken record. "And Chicago?"

"There's a folder full of bank transactions, a couple of years' worth. There were only about four or five variations in the numbers." She paused to see if Cassie followed her train of thought. When Harris was met with silence, she continued. "The files read like services rendered. A flat fee for a project completed. The night of David's murder is on that list."

"Services rendered?" Cassie didn't like the way her mind was putting two and two together. "You're talking about an assassin?"

Harris shrugged, looking far too casual for the topic at hand. "Someone murdered David with a police-issue sniper rifle. It was a professional job. So, yes, it makes sense."

"Let me get this straight." Cassie's teeth rattled, and she wasn't sure it was just from the cold. "We're in Chicago, following a lead on the *assassin* who killed David?" No matter how many times she said *assassin*, it didn't make the word any easier to swallow. "Does that not sound insane to you?"

"We're following the money trail. If this person is doing jobs for Aguilar, they could be anywhere—Savannah, Chicago, Tallahassee, Rome."

"You think Aguilar needs to take care of business in Rome?"

"No, but the point still stands. I doubt we'll run into David's killer unless we sound the alarms, and we're trying to avoid that." Frustration flashed across Harris's face. "We have a bunch of numbers in a bunch of files, but nothing tied to physical evidence. That's why we're here. We need to figure out where that money went and prove it was a payoff for David's murder."

"You mentioned an address?"

Harris bobbed her head. They were approaching the end of the path, and yet another fountain rose in the distance. "I imagine Sherman put together the information on the flash drive quickly, hoping to offload it to David and get out of Dodge as soon as he could. Some folders make more sense than others. This one didn't have much context, but he had included an address. I figure that's where we start."

Cassie stopped at the foot of the fountain and looked up into the metallic face of the sixteenth president of the United States. *Abraham Lincoln: The Man* was cast in 1887 and stood twelve feet tall. It depicted the former leader rising from a chair, preparing to give a speech. Holding his lapel, he looks down in contemplation. As with most representations of the historical figure, the statue exudes an air of regality and quiet intelligence.

Looking into his face reminded Cassie of Lincoln's complex history. Though many consider him the Great Emancipator, historical evidence suggested that while the president didn't agree with the institution of slavery, he also didn't view Black Americans as equal. As beloved as Lincoln is, and as wonderful as his accomplishments have been, he was still human—full of flaws, contradictions, and secrets.

Cassie turned to Harris. "David left me a letter."

The detective's eyes widened. "When?"

"I'm not sure when he wrote it. Lisa gave it to me the day of the funeral."

Harris hesitated. "You never told me."

"I didn't open it right away." Cassie found it hard to swallow past the lump in her throat. "I wasn't sure what to expect. But that last day in New Orleans, I decided to see what it said."

Harris's voice was soft. "You don't have to tell me."

"David wanted me to." A pressure settled into Cassie's chest, and she had to fight to get enough air to speak. "He wanted me to tell you this wasn't your fault. He knew what he was getting into."

Harris blinked rapidly. When she spoke, her voice wavered. "I don't understand."

"Neither do I." Cassie fought her own tears. "I don't know what he was talking about. But he said he wanted his secrets to stay buried with him. He wanted me to tell you to let it go."

"Let it go?" Harris's voice was no longer soft. "Why?"

"He said it would be better than the truth." Cassie fought the mounting force threatening to steal the air from her lungs. "I've never heard him talk this way before." Her voice shook. "I'm scared."

Harris looked down at her shoes. Cassie could see the gears turning in her head. "You're here, which means you won't try to talk me out of following this lead."

"No," Cassie said. "I won't."

"We're in this together." Harris looked up. A tear had slid down her cheek and she didn't bother to wipe it away. "Right?"

Cassie didn't answer immediately. Harris's question wasn't a small one. David's final request meant something to her, and the last thing she wanted was to be disloyal to her friends, in life or death. But he had gotten himself mixed up in something big. And he hadn't told Cassie. The sting of betrayal battled against her fear of learning the truth.

There was no other person on the planet she had revered and respected as much as David, but he was still human—full of flaws, contradictions, and secrets. The prospect of digging up his skeletons terrified her, but now that she knew they existed, she couldn't imagine a life where she wouldn't spend every waking moment wondering where they came from.

Cassie gazed into Lincoln's face and then over at Harris. Their eyes met, and Cassie knew her answer.

"There's no turning back now."

4

Harris's car rental—a gold 2012 Toyota Corolla—was hideous and smelled like an abandoned Burger King.

After throwing her duffel in the trunk and slipping inside, Cassie stopped short of checking under her seat for stale fries or a lost pickle. She didn't want to know what the center console looked like. If her own was any indication, the compartment was better left to its own devices.

The detective didn't seem to mind. She didn't say anything about the car to comment on either the color or the smell. It wasn't exactly 24-karat, but Cassie didn't feel inconspicuous. Or sanitary.

"Do we know anything about this address?" Cassie tried to keep the apprehension out of her voice. She trusted Harris, but there was no denying they were going off half-cocked here. "Anything at all?"

"I looked it up beforehand, don't worry." Harris must've picked up on her doubt. "It's a jewelry store. Completely ordinary."

"Something tells me you don't believe that."

Harris smirked. "It's a legitimate business with a website and a phone number. Even had a handful of testimonials. Apparently, they have great customer service. But yeah, if it's listed on that flash drive, it likely serves another purpose."

"I had a feeling. What do you think's going on?"

Harris shrugged. She pulled to a stop at a light and looked over at Cassie. "My first thought was money laundering. They set up a legitimate jewelry store and someone comes in to buy one of the items with stolen or counterfeit money. Now it's part of the system." The light turned green, and she hit the gas. "Let's say they buy a diamond bracelet. That represents the cash they gave their contact at the store. Now they go to another shop—probably a second jewelry store, pawn shop, or private collector. The store owner buys the bracelet for an agreed upon price—"

"The amount they bought the bracelet for at the other shop."

"Minus a service fee, of course. And now the thief has clean cash, and the store owner has a new piece to sell to their own people. The whole transaction is backed up with a purchase history and proof of authenticity."

"And the original stolen cash?"

"Same deal. Someone comes in with a piece of jewelry and the cash is split between sales. Now it looks totally ordinary. Police have a harder time tracking it if it ends up in a couple dozen places across the country, and they can't blame the business for making a transaction."

"Wouldn't the police figure it out sooner or later?" Cassie asked. "That the jewelry store is just a front?"

Harris laughed, and Cassie felt the heat of embarrassment creep up her neck. "First of all, this is Chicago. There's plenty of corruption to go around. Half the cops are getting paid off to look the other way. And that's being generous." Harris flipped the turn signal up and took a right. Cassie had no idea where they were. Every street looked the same. "But even if they think the jewelry store is a front, they'd need evidence to get a warrant for a raid. And even if they raided the place, there's no guarantee they'd find the money. The turnover rate is high for these places."

"What happens if a regular person walks in and wants to buy something?"

Harris took a left down a one-way street and pulled over. "Their prices are gonna be high, but there are people who'd rather pay for an overpriced item to ensure the quality. The good money launderers will make sure their shop is full of real pieces." She popped her door open. "Come on. We can walk the rest of the way."

Cassie climbed out of the car, folding her arms across her chest as if to shrink herself small enough to avoid the assaulting wind. The biting cold nipped at her nose, and she wished she'd thought to buy a scarf.

The sidewalks were clear of snow, but she stepped lightly, knowing the last thing she needed was to hit a patch of black ice and break her leg. Then she'd definitely be missing more work.

The two of them looked like a pair of friends out for a lunchtime stroll. Cassie wondered what the people inside the store would think. That they were potential patrons? That they might be there to clean their own cash? Criminals were made of all sorts of people. But a part of her wondered if they'd see Harris for what she really was.

Not that it'd be easy. In her long coat and Timberlands, Harris looked like a Chicago native. It was obvious she'd grown up in the cold weather—her jacket flapped open with the breeze, and there wasn't a goosebump in sight. Her rosy cheeks made her look bright and healthy compared to the Harris who had slumped into Cassie's house back in Savannah, half-drunk off misery and guilt.

They turned a corner, and the detective pulled up short. The jewelry store stood in front of them, on the corner of a side street that didn't have much foot traffic. Convenient for a business that wanted to stay out of the spotlight, and great for real patrons who thought they'd found a hidden gem.

But it wasn't meant to be.

A large CLOSED sign hung in the plywood-covered window. Caution tape draped across the front door. Harris pushed her aviators to the top of her head to get a better look. Then she took a step forward and tried the handle. Locked. Cassie heard her curse under her breath.

"Dead end?" Cassie asked, trying not to sound hopeful.

"Let's go around back."

Harris retraced their steps, and Cassie followed. Back around the corner, they turned into a darkened alleyway. If the hardened snow on the ground meant anything, it was that the sun barely found its way back there. The ice crunched underfoot, but Cassie observed plenty of footprints marring the path. No one would notice an extra set or two.

When they reached the back door to the jewelry shop, Harris nudged it open with the toe of her boot. She looked back at Cassie with raised eyebrows. It felt like an invitation, one Cassie didn't feel compelled to accept. But there was no stopping Harris now that they had some semblance of a lead. The detective crossed the threshold and entered the building, and Cassie followed once again.

The shop was larger than Cassie would've thought. Several huge glass display cases cut the room in half, with a few smaller ones near the front of the store. She had half expected the glass to be shattered and the room demolished, but they were whole. And empty. It might not have been a break-in, but someone had definitely cleaned house. They'd left behind some papers scattered across the floor and a handful of filing cabinets. Two other doors stood wide open, leading to back rooms. She could see more papers. More filing cabinets. A few pieces of furniture.

The shop was still warm, despite the back door not having been closed all the way, and Cassie unbuttoned her jacket, glad to have a reprieve from the outside air. But something felt off. A hot, cloying hand wrapped itself around her chest, and every time she took a breath, it squeezed tighter. "I think we're in the right place."

"Yeah?" Harris sounded distracted. She was already combing through the debris on the floor. "What makes you say that?"

"You know. Just a feeling."

"If anyone else said that, I'd have them committed." She stood up, giving Cassie her full attention. "What kind of feeling?"

"Unsettled. Uncomfortable."

Harris went back to the search. "Well, that clears it up."

Cassie stripped off her jacket. "Is it hot in here, or is it just me?"

"Just you." Harris pulled open one of the drawers to the filing cabinet, but it was empty. So was the next one. When she pulled the third one open and found more of the same, she huffed in frustration. "We're too late." But she moved onto the next room anyway.

Cassie hung back, making her way through at a slower pace. She pulled her phone out and started taking pictures of each room, of the different cases and various filing cabinets. Of all the papers on the floor. The heat slowed her down, distracted her. But maybe something here could help and they just didn't know it yet. Maybe it could serve as evidence.

Ten minutes later, neither of them had found anything useful, and Cassie felt sweat dripping down her back. She peeled off her chunky sweater and draped it over her arm with her coat. Now she stood there in a tank top and jeans. She'd been cursing Chicago's winter air all morning, and now it was all she wanted.

Cassie entered the last room and raised her phone. Harris blinked in the flash of Cassie's final picture. There wasn't much in there. A rickety metal desk and folding chair sat in the corner. It barely looked functional, let alone comfortable. It could've been a real office, but Cassie got the feeling it had just been for show.

"Did you see anything?" Harris asked. She looked Cassie up and down. "Are you okay?"

"You're really not hot?" Cassie asked.

"Not even a little bit."

Cassie tried blowing her hair out of her face, but it stuck to the sweat on her brow. "No, I didn't see anything."

"This doesn't disprove my theory about the jewelry store being a front." She walked back out to the main room. "It clearly wasn't a robbery. They cleared it out on purpose. All the furniture is second-hand. The papers on the floor"—she kicked at a pamphlet—"are either garbage or props to make it look more legitimate."

"So, they knew we were coming?"

"Maybe not *us*," Harris said. "But they knew it was time to pack up and leave. We just have to figure out why." She peered at Cassie like she was weighing options. Then she gestured to the pile of clothes in her arms. "What's going on with you?"

"I don't know, but if I don't get out of here soon, I'm going to pass out." The hand around her chest gave her a final squeeze. "Or turn into soup."

Harris chewed the inside of her cheek, as if debating the pros and cons of having a liquefied partner. But she must've decided it wasn't worth it. "Let's go grab some lunch. I doubt they'll come back for a bunch of empty filing cabinets." She paused in the doorway. "I was going to suggest soup, but now that seems cannibalistic."

Cassie didn't argue. There was something off about this place, but she could hardly think straight. The heat had infiltrated every brain cell, burning her up from the inside. Against her better judgment, she slipped her sweater over her head but left her coat hanging off her arm. By the time she made it back outside, the air felt like a cool salve against her feverish skin.

5

Zbirak had booked the cheapest motel room he could find. For less than forty-five dollars a night, he had a door with a deadbolt, heavy curtains, a shower, and the luxury of only having to walk through the front door twice—once to pick up his key and once to drop it back off. This was the type of place that took cash and didn't ask questions.

It was perfect.

As a bonus, his room contained two twin beds. The duvets were hideous, of course. Mauve and teal and mustard petals floated across the cover as though pushed by an invisible wind. He'd spent enough time in hotel rooms to know they rarely washed the bedspread. Balling them up, he threw them in the closet. The sheets were stiff and scratchy, but at least they looked clean.

One bed was for sleeping. He subsisted on four hours every night. When he was a teenager, he had optimized his body.

It had started with consuming a precise number of calories every day. He had always been thin and wiry, so weight was not an issue. But he needed muscle. Enough to overpower his enemies without slowing him down. Nine times out of ten, his speed gave him the upper hand in a fight. But that other ten percent wasn't to be ignored.

His slight frame was a smokescreen for the power he had stored in his muscles. He could easily restrain a person twice his size.

Then, he trained his sleep schedule to follow a simple pattern. Going to bed at the same time every night and waking up five minutes earlier every day. If he overslept, he'd start over at the beginning. Now, he could fall asleep within sixty seconds and wake up within four hours. No more, no less. He was a light sleeper, but thanks to his regimen, he always felt well-rested. How many people could claim that?

The other bed was for his partner. His arsenal. He chuckled to the empty room. He had met many killers throughout his lifetime, but few saw their weapons as anything more than tools to aid in their chosen vocation. Not him. He saw his guns, his knives, his poisons as friends. If you treated them well, you would gain their loyalty. They would never betray you. If a mission went sideways, you only had yourself to blame. A leader should always take responsibility for his team. And Zbirak took his responsibilities very seriously.

After laying out his arsenal, he took stock of his weapons. There was a missing spot at the corner of the bed, grid thirty-two, where a vial of poison should have been. His friend had served him well tonight, dispatching Officer Pisano with ease. A loyal servant to the cause—right up until the end.

In a few days, Zbirak would make a new friend. Grid thirty-two would be filled. The team would be complete once more.

Until then, there was work to do. Zbirak showered, getting the stink of Pisano off his skin. Changing clothes, he dumped his old outfit into the bathtub to light it on fire. With the window open and the door shut with a towel against the space along the bottom, the smoke detector never even knew of the danger.

When his clothes were nothing more than ash and ribbons, and the smoke had cleared, he gathered the remnants into a bag and placed them in a dumpster behind the motel.

Returning to his room, Zbirak turned on the television and clicked through the channels until he found the news. Starting with his rifle, he broke down each of his weapons, cleaning them with the ease and familiarity of an old friend.

Atlanta had its fair share of crime, and he did not expect any of the local reporters to have found Pisano's story so soon. Still, it never hurt to check. He liked being in the know, up to speed on who was chasing him and why. For now, the Atlanta PD was blissfully unaware of his presence in their city, and he hoped to be gone by the time they decided to look for him.

Zbirak set his rifle back into its position on the bed and picked up his pistol. He was only half paying attention, but the movements were second nature. He could do it blindfolded. He could do it in his sleep.

No, most of his brain power was directed toward finding a solution to his current problem.

Pisano had let Mrs. Sherman slip through his fingers. What had been one loose thread had quickly turned into three. These things had a way of spiraling out of control, but Zbirak had clipped the man and his nephew. He was back down to one. By now, she would know her time was coming to an end. An ordinary woman, Mrs. Sherman had proven herself to be resourceful. She had evaded all his—albeit passive—attempts to capture her thus far.

This allowed Zbirak to come to several conclusions. One, Mrs. Sherman had known the nature of her husband's work. Two, she understood the consequences of severing ties with their employer. And three, Mrs. Sherman was adaptable. She had once relied on the police—which is why Zbirak had sent Pisano to bring her in—but his sources told him she had become uncooperative before going off the grid. Pisano's nephew had driven her away, and now Zbirak suffered the consequences.

If he could kill that man a second time, he would not hesitate.

But as smart as Mrs. Sherman was, she did not have a lot of resources. In trying times, people either turned to the authorities or whoever they trusted most. Who did the woman trust? A family member? A longtime friend? He didn't know much about her personal life, but a quick trip back to Savannah would give him the answers he needed.

As if on cue, his cell phone rang. Only two people had this phone number, and Zbirak didn't need to see the caller ID to know which it was.

"Hello?"

"Joseph." The voice was congenial. Too familiar. Grating. "Did you have a good night?"

"I had to send my steak back to the kitchen, but otherwise it was" —he searched for the right word—"fruitful."

"Good. I have another problem here in Savannah I'd like you to take care of."

"I had every intention of stopping by when I got into town." Zbirak's voice was pleasant enough, but his hackles were raised. He didn't like starting a new job before the last one was finished. His employer knew that. "But—"

"Before you get your panties in a bunch, it's familiar territory." There was a dark chuckle on the other end before the voice turned serious. "Consider it an apology for my impatience. I should've waited for you to begin with."

"Oh?"

"Another loose end." It didn't clarify much, but Zbirak knew he'd be getting his answers tomorrow. "And something tells me you'll enjoy trimming this one."

Zbirak smiled. His line of business didn't allow him to trust people, and although he had little in common with his current employer, the man had gone out of his way to make sure Zbirak knew he respected his talents. An extra job was no hardship to maintain a relationship like that.

Zbirak had been silent for too long. "As a bonus," the man said, "I'll buy you the best damn steak you'll ever eat."

Zbirak's smile widened. "Deal."

6

AFTER WALKING A BLOCK FROM THE UNINHABITED JEWELRY STORE, Cassie's internal temperature returned to normal. Donning her jacket, she stuck her hands in the pockets, already chilled to the bone.

What happened in the jewelry story was supernatural, but what did it mean? She hadn't seen anything—no ghosts, no visions, no shadows moving out of the corner of her eye. Whatever the other side was trying to tell her, it wasn't getting through.

Harris drove them a few blocks to a small restaurant named Tommy's. It sold sandwiches, soups, and a single cobb salad. The detective got a bowl of chowder large enough to feed three. Cassie got the salad. They requested a small table in the back, jammed against the wall. The lunch hour crowd was loud and boisterous, but Cassie enjoyed it after the jewelry store's oppressive silence.

"So." Cassie lifted a forkful of lettuce smothered in blue cheese dressing to her mouth. "What now?"

Harris shrugged and slurped her soup. She seemed forcibly cavalier about the fact that they had hit a dead end. Like she was willing to do anything but admit they'd already lost their best lead. "Gotta figure out where the jewelry store owner went." She pulled out her phone. "Either that or go through the flash drive and find another address."

Cassie stuffed another bite of food into her mouth, afraid that if she spoke, she'd say something she'd regret. They'd only been at this for an hour or two, but she was ready to give up hope. Maybe it was a gut feeling, or maybe it was guilt over ignoring David's final wishes. But Harris wasn't going to let go of this until they found something.

But what if they found something Harris didn't want to know?

Cassie pulled out her own phone and flipped through the photos of the jewelry store. She wondered what the people around her thought—two young women on their phones instead of talking to each other. Typical Millennials. If only they had any idea what these women were here for.

Cassie swiped to the next photo. Nothing out of the ordinary. The room was full of empty cases. Pamphlets and litter on the floor. The unused filing cabinets. If they had at least found *something*, maybe this wouldn't feel like a lost cause. Cassie took another bite of salad, then flipped to the next photo, and—

She gasped around a mouthful of food. "Holy shit."

Harris looked up. "What?"

Cassie forced the food down her throat. "I'm not sure."

Harris made a frustrated sound. "Well, you said that for a reason."

"I mean," Cassie said, leveling her with a glare, "I'm not sure what I'm looking at."

"Pictures from the jewelry store?"

Cassie nodded. "I took them in case we needed to look back at something."

Harris must've gotten tired of her beating around the bush because she pushed her chair out as far as it would go—about four inches—and came around to Cassie's side of the table, not caring that she was now towering over the older couple to their left. She leaned down for a closer look. "Is this the filing cabinet in the second room?"

"Yeah, the one in the corner." Cassie leaned forward, too. Their heads were almost touching. "I didn't notice this at the time."

Next to the black, beat-up, metal filing cabinet was a shadow.

Darker than it should've been, like it had some mass to it. In fact, it almost looked solid and three-dimensional, as though it weren't simply resting against the wall, but stepping away from it. From this angle, Cassie couldn't tell whether it was a man's or a woman's. But it wasn't hers—which was off to the left side of the picture.

"Where was I when you took this?" Harris asked.

"The third room. I just popped my head in here for a minute." She swiped forward to the next picture. This one focused on the other side of the room. But you could still see the filing cabinet. And the shadow.

"We have to go back," Harris said.

Cassie looked up at her. "Wait. We don't even know if this is something worth investigating."

"Everything is worth investigating." Harris was already looking for the waitress. "You felt your temperature rise in there. Then you see the shadow and freak out."

"I didn't freak out."

"You were *startled*." She caught the gaze of their server and mimed signing the check. The woman flashed them a wide smile and held up a finger before heading back into the kitchen. "You think this is something, too."

"Will you just sit down?" Cassie leaned forward. "It's not what you think."

Harris settled into the chair opposite her with an exasperated huff. When Cassie didn't speak right away, Harris gestured for Cassie to go on.

Cassie took a deep breath. She didn't know what to say. Didn't even know where to start. "Something weird happened in New Orleans."

"No offense, but you're usually the something weird."

Cassie rolled her eyes. "Jason and I met this woman, Sabine Delacroix. She took us to one of the cemeteries."

"Normal couple outing."

"We're not a couple."

Harris raised an eyebrow but didn't say anything.

"While we were there, she took us to the center of the cemetery. Then she did, um, something."

"Did what?"

"Opened the veil?" Cassie couldn't help that it came out like a question.

"The veil? What does that even mean?"

"To the other side."

"The other side of wh—" Harris's eyes grew wide. "You mean, like, heaven?"

Cassie shook her head. "The other side, as in the spirit world. It's not heaven. More like limbo."

"Purgatory?"

She shrugged. "Call it whatever you want. For me, it's always been like a curtain that hangs between our world and theirs."

"Theirs? You mean ghosts."

"Yeah. Our worlds exist over the top of each other's. Restless spirits stick around here until they find what they're looking for, whether it's justice or peace or whatever." Cassie took a sip of her water. Her tongue felt as dry as a desert. "Then they go to the other side. In my experience, they usually stay there."

"I feel a *but* coming on," Harris said.

"In that cemetery, I literally saw the curtain pulled back. That's never happened before. I've never been able to peer through the veil."

"What did you see?"

Cassie looked down at her phone. "A shadow."

"That's it? A shadow?" Harris didn't bother hiding her disappointment. "Is that important?"

"At the time, I thought the shadow could be David."

That caught Harris's attention. "What made you think that?"

"I don't know. Whoever it was, they either didn't want me to see their face, or something else was keeping them from reaching out to me."

It was Harris's turn to look down at the phone. "So, you think this is David?"

"I don't know—" Cassie broke off when the waitress arrived with their check.

"Thanks." Harris beamed as she handed over her card and sent the server away again.

Cassie barely had a chance to reach into her purse. "I could've paid for my own."

Harris waved her away. "Are you sure it's not David?"

"I'm not sure of anything." Cassie took another sip of water. "But I do think it's weird I saw someone covered in shadow in New Orleans, and now here I am seeing another shadow in Chicago."

"There's no reason to *not* think it's him." She leaned forward. "We're investigating his murder. It would make sense."

Cassie regretted even bringing it up. Harris wouldn't listen to reason now. "Adelaide—"

"We have to go back." The fire in Harris's eyes battled against the tears that had gathered in the corners. "We have to make sure."

7

THE STREETS IN THIS NEIGHBORHOOD WERE AT LEAST STARTING TO LOOK familiar. Cassie still had no idea where she was in Chicago—though she did remember seeing the sign for Market Street—but she trusted Harris to get them where they needed to go. The detective didn't even use her phone to navigate, and Cassie couldn't figure out if she'd memorized their route prior to coming to the city or if she just knew Chicago as well as she knew Savannah.

Harris barely put the car in park before she swung open her door and marched toward the shop. Cassie jogged to keep up, unbuttoning her jacket in anticipation of feeling the invisible tendrils of flame licking at her skin. But as they got closer, the sensation never arrived.

The detective stopped when she got to the back door. It was wide open.

"Didn't we close it?" Cassie asked. Their brisk walk had caused the question to come out through gasps.

Harris pulled out the gun she'd hidden under her jacket at the back of her waistband. "Stay behind me."

"Where did you get that?" Cassie hissed. "Aren't you suspended?"

"This one's mine," Harris said with a fondness in her voice. "Not police-issued."

Cassie wasn't sure how that made her feel. She was no stranger to guns or gunfights at this point, but she didn't love the idea of being caught in the middle of yet another standoff. She trusted Harris with her life, but Cassie admitted the detective's one-track mind concerned her.

Harris didn't wait for Cassie's approval. She slipped into the building with her gun ready, but not fully raised. As an off-duty cop in a different city—in a different state—breaking and entering with a loaded weapon could be grounds for serious disciplinary action. Not just here, but also back home.

Cassie only hesitated for a few seconds before following Harris inside. She expected to be hit with the same wall of heat she had felt earlier, but the shop was as cold as the outside. Was it because the door had been left open? Had the cold air seeped inside, or had whatever caused the heat finally escaped?

Whatever it was, Cassie didn't have time to explore her options. She flattened herself against the wall and followed in Harris's footsteps. Her eyes darted around the room and her ears strained to hear anything out of the ordinary. The front room didn't look any different than it had before. And it was still dead silent.

Still, the air felt like it had shifted in the last hour. Cassie couldn't put her finger on it, let alone find the words to describe it to Harris. The cold penetrated her sweatshirt, so she buttoned her coat against it, confused, grateful, and a little disappointed that whatever had been here before was now gone.

Harris made her way along the wall and turned into the room on the right. Cassie peeked her head in and noticed the metal desk and chair were gone. "It was empty, though," she whispered. Harris held a finger to her lips and kept moving.

The room ahead was also empty. The remaining filing cabinets were gone, including the one the shadow had been standing beside. Harris cleared the room, then lowered her weapon. She turned back to Cassie. "Anything?"

Cassie pulled out her phone and snapped a picture of the general area where the cabinet had been. When she looked down, there was no shadow. Not even a suspicious dust particle floating through the air. Cassie shook her head. "Nothing. The shadow's either gone or—"

"Was tied to that filing cabinet." Harris started for the doorway. "We need to find out where it went."

"Wait, Adelaide." Cassie was nervous, and not just because someone had been here while they were at lunch. An absence in the building set her on edge. "We don't even know if it was important. Or related to this case."

"You're right, we don't know." She looked over her shoulder at Cassie. "So, we need to find out."

Cassie opened her mouth to respond—to say what, she wasn't sure—when they heard the back door to the store open again. Male voices infiltrated the room, and before Cassie could comprehend what was happening, Harris had pushed her around the corner and against the wall with one arm and raised her weapon with the other.

"Come on, man. Just pick one. It isn't rocket surgery," one man said.

"I think you mean rocket science," the other replied.

"That's the joke, dude. Seriously?"

During the beat of silence, Cassie kept her eyes trained on Harris to see what the detective would do. She wanted to believe these guys were just concerned citizens, but the first man sounded older and tougher, like he'd been around the block a few times. His voice was ragged, both from his walk to the store and from years of cigarette usage. As soon as Cassie thought it, she could smell the smoke wafting toward them.

The second voice sounded younger. Hesitant and maybe even scared, like he was nervous but trying to prove his mettle. He wanted to make an impression and was weighing his options. Trying to figure out what the right answer was. Cassie could hear the heat of shame creeping into his voice.

"If I had to choose between only eating tacos or only eating pizza for the rest of my life, I would choose pizza." The shame was quickly replaced with pride. "Because I could also get a taco pizza. You can't have a pizza taco, can you?"

"A pizza taco is basically a calzone."

Harris and Cassie exchanged a look. This wasn't exactly the conversation of a pair of criminal masterminds, but for the life of her, Cassie couldn't figure out why the two men were here and what they wanted. And what it had to do with pizza or tacos.

"I think pizza is a better medium for taco ingredients. A calzone isn't exactly—"

"Dude, really?" The first man paused and then breathed out. Cassie imagined him blowing cigarette smoke into the kid's face in annoyance. "It's not that deep. Let's just get the rest of this stuff and get out of here. I got shit to do today."

"Why do they need this junk, anyway? It's not worth anything."

"Boss said—"

As their voices neared, Cassie took an involuntary step backwards. The floor creaked, and the first man cut off. There was a hushed silence. All four of them held their breath. A shiver went down Cassie's spine that had nothing to do with the temperature in the room. Harris didn't bother shooting her a look, but Cassie could feel the frustration radiating off her.

"What was that?" the kid asked.

The only indication that the other man had made a move was another creak of the floorboard. But it was enough of a warning for Harris to anticipate him coming around the corner, and as soon as his foot crossed the threshold into the room, she rushed forward.

Cassie watched as Harris brought her knee up into the man's groin. He was younger than Cassie had imagined, but still around ten years older than them. He was thin and tanned and wore a ratty baseball hat and a scraggly beard. His fingers and neck were tattooed, which she could see peeking out from under his sweatshirt.

The man's eyes went wide as he grabbed his crotch. Harris wasted no time elbowing him in the side of the head, which sent him sprawling across the floor. He landed like a sack of flour, and Harris was already on top of him, her knee pressed into his back.

A noise made Cassie turn, and she locked eyes with the young kid. Now that she got a good look at him, she couldn't imagine he was

eighteen yet. He still had a layer of baby fat in his face and a wispy ·
mustache stood out against his bronze skin. He was tall—at least six
feet—with a hint of muscle under a bulky coat. He probably could've
shoved Cassie to the side and gotten the upper hand with Harris, but
the fear in his eyes told her the thought hadn't even occurred to him.
And before she could say anything, he turned and sprinted out the
door.

Cassie looked back to Harris, who was struggling to keep the
writhing man beneath her. She was sweating with effort, but as she
yanked his arm up farther along his back, he quieted down. She
locked eyes with Cassie as the kid bolted.

"Don't let him get away," she barked, then turned her attention
back to the first man.

Cassie had no choice. Despite her better judgment, she took off
running after the boy.

Of course, she had no idea what she'd do if she caught up to the
kid. Harris was likely thinking the same thing she was—the younger
man would be easier to interrogate than the older one.

But she had to catch him first.

Cassie burst through the back door and skidded across the alleyway. In the last hour, the ice and snow had melted into a thick slurry
that provided no traction for her boots. But the cold wind on her face
woke her up, even if the sun's bright light blinded her temporarily. As
she blinked away the spots in her vision, she caught sight of one of
the kid's shoes just as he turned the corner. She sped after him, hot
on his heels.

The kid was fast, but he wasted valuable energy checking over his
shoulder every couple of seconds. Cassie thanked God for the traction on her boots. She wasn't exactly an all-star athlete, but she tried
to stay in shape. Still, her lungs burned, and her eyes watered from
the cold wind whipping her face. She refused to blink away the tears,
afraid she'd lose sight of her target.

"Stop!" She was going for commanding, but it came out desperate. "Wait! We just want to talk!"

The kid didn't listen. He put his head down and whipped around the next corner. They were about a block away from the jewelry store now, heading in the opposite direction from Harris's rental car, and Cassie started to panic. What if there were others? Harris had taken the larger threat, but there was no guarantee Cassie wasn't getting herself into a worse situation.

Just as Cassie turned the corner, she realized she'd been led into a trap. The kid was waiting there for her, his elbow out and aimed at her diaphragm. When it connected, all the air whooshed out of her lungs. The pain caused her vision to go white, and she collapsed to her knees. She raised a hand to protect her face, unsure of what he planned to do next. Knock her out? Pull a weapon and threaten her? He was clearly afraid, but he could still go on the offensive. And she was at a severe disadvantage.

Luckily for her, he had no intention of hurting her. As Cassie gathered her senses, still wheezing from the lack of oxygen in her lungs, she watched as the kid sprinted down the block and jumped into a plain white box truck. Cassie had just enough time to pull out her phone and zoom into the license plate to take a picture before he hit the gas.

Their biggest lead now barreled down the street in the opposite direction, and Cassie slumped against the cold façade of whatever building she'd landed against, not even caring that the snow was seeping into her jeans, freezing her to the bone.

8

IF HARRIS HAD HER HANDCUFFS, THERE WAS NO WAY THE GUY ON THE floor would've escaped.

But she didn't have them, and he was a slippery son of a bitch. Freeing one arm, he whipped it around, connecting with her shoulder where she'd been shot a couple days prior. Pain flared down her arm, and the man took advantage of her distraction, jumped to his feet, and dashed to the door. He slammed it shut behind him, forcing her to take time wrenching it back open. Once she made it outside, he had a sizable lead on her.

She refused to give up. They were so close to some sort of answer. Unfortunately, the man in front of her seemed to be fighting for his life. Whether he thought she was a cop or not didn't matter. He was willing to run instead of fight, and that gave her two assumptions: He was a coward, or the information he had was more important than his pride.

Despite his thin legs, the man was fast, and Harris had trouble keeping up, especially in the slush-filled alleyway. Once they hit the sidewalk, she had better traction, but so did he. No matter how much she pumped her arms, he pumped his faster. Not many people could outrun her at a dead sprint, but this guy looked like he'd been a track star in his youth. The cigarettes apparently hadn't done any damage to his lung capacity.

As they neared the next corner, Harris saw Cassie slumped on the ground, her head leaning back against the outside wall of a building. Harris's heart shuddered to a stop, then started beating in double time. The kid hadn't seemed like that big of a threat—he'd looked too afraid to be dangerous. Had she underestimated him? Harris hadn't known Cassie for very long, but the thought of losing her after having just lost David sent her into a spiral. Her vision darkened along the edges as Cassie's body became the sole focus of her tunnel vision.

The man never stopped running. Launching himself over Cassie's outstretched legs, he veered into the street. A white box truck slammed on its brakes, and the man jumped inside. The door hadn't even closed before they took off again. Her closest lead disappeared down the road in a haze of exhaust.

Harris knelt next to Cassie. Now that she was closer, she could see Cassie's eyes were open and focused. She was breathing hard and rubbing her chest, but otherwise seemed fine. Harris was relieved and frustrated and angry all at once. More at herself than anyone. How had this happened?

Cassie looked up at Harris, her red hair frizzy from the winter air and her sprint down the sidewalk. Her cheeks were flushed, making her freckles stand out even more than usual. There was the quirk of a smile on her lips, masking her pain. "Hey."

Harris felt a bubble of laughter try to escape her mouth. Clamping down on it, her lips still twitched upward ever so slightly. "Hi. You okay?"

Cassie pointed to her chest. "Ouch."

"What happened?" Harris scooped her arms under Cassie's and pulled the other woman to her feet. "Anything broken?"

"Not broken. Just bruised." She still sounded out of breath, but it was returning to normal. "He elbowed me as I came around the corner and I fell." Cassie looked around like she expected to see the other guy hog-tied on the sidewalk. "Where's yours?"

Harris gestured toward the truck, which was just a white speck in the distance now. "Gone."

"Least it wasn't just me."

"Not just you," Harris said, and this time she couldn't keep the annoyance out of her voice. "Back to square one."

"Not exactly." Cassie raised her hand, grasping her cell phone. On the screen was a grainy but legible picture of the white van's license plate. When Harris looked back up at her with wide eyes, Cassie grinned. "I win."

"Yes, you do." This could be enough to get them back on the right path. Harris pulled out her own phone. "Now we just have to call it in."

"Aren't you suspended?"

This time Harris let the smile spread over her face. "I have my ways." Then her smile dropped as she realized how she'd have to get the information they needed. "But this is something I need to do on my own."

If Cassie had questions, she didn't ask them. Rubbing her chest, she said, "I need a distraction, anyway."

Rather than standing on the cold street, Harris dropped Cassie back off at the Chicago History Museum. Harris had nothing against museums, but she didn't revere them the way Cassie did. Most people didn't.

But this was as good a place as any to make her phone call. Harris walked down the paths surrounding the museum, where she had met Cassie earlier that day. The brisk air felt good on her flushed faced. But the flush was from more than embarrassment. It was shame. She hadn't mentioned this to Cassie—or anyone, for that matter—but Harris had burned a lot of her bridges already. Following David's death, she'd called in as many favors as she could. She hadn't exactly asked nicely, which meant more than a few of her contacts told her not to call again. At least she still had one person guaranteed to pick up the phone.

But even his kindness was running thin.

Harris found a bench but didn't sit. It was too cold for that.

Pulling out her phone, she paced back and forth, staring at the Montana area code and wishing she were home. She missed her family and friends. The ones who still talked to her, anyway. But out of everyone on the entire planet, she missed Hector the most.

When he picked up, his soft voice was cold. "What do you need, Adelaide?"

"Can't a lady just—"

"No."

Harris pictured Hector leaning over his keyboard, his head ducked low, hoping no one would catch him on his cell. At one point in time, they had been best friends. She had moved to Savannah for a promotion, and he'd stayed in Montana. He had always known who he was, had always seen what his future held.

Harris was jealous sometimes. Since moving to the South, she felt like she'd become a different person. Not better or worse, not more herself or less. Just different. She had different priorities now, different interests. She and Hector had drifted apart. In the past year or two, they hadn't even wished each other a happy birthday. She started to promise herself that she'd do better, like she always did when she thought of him, but what was the point? She'd just get wrapped up in something else and forget about him again.

And it wasn't like he was knocking down her door to talk to her, either.

"I need you to run a plate for me."

"You know I can't—"

"Yes, you can." Harris tried to keep the apathy out of her voice. She didn't like this version of herself—the one who was more interested in getting the job done than keeping up appearances. She could fake small talk with anyone but him. Hector had always been able to see right through her. "It's important."

"It's always important." His voice was louder, and she could hear him attempting to control the anger. "What about the other stuff that's important? What about me? I was happy to help when I thought you cared—"

"I do care." She hated the way her voice shook. She was better than this. Stronger. "I've always cared. I just—" A sob escaped. All she could see was David's body, lying there. Dead.

Silence enveloped the other end of the line. Harris worried he'd hung up, but then she heard him sigh into the receiver. "What's going on?"

"A friend of mine was murdered." She took a deep breath. The cold stung her lungs, but it cleared her mind. She blinked away the tears. But she couldn't control the sniffling. "He was a cop. I'm in Chicago running down a lead."

"Chicago?" Hector clicked his tongue in approval. "Did you go to Tommy's?"

"Of course." She laughed, but it came out wet with emotion. "The place has changed a lot. Not even the same owner anymore, I don't think. Chowder was just okay."

"Well, it's been twelve years. Things are bound to change."

"Yeah." It was all Harris could say. Suddenly, she felt like the one who'd been elbowed in the chest. "I'm sorry."

"I know." Hector cleared his throat. "I'm sorry, too. About your friend."

It didn't feel like he'd forgiven her, but he was trying. "Thank you."

"What's the plate?"

Harris had memorized it the second she'd seen the picture. "Seven, three, nine, six, Delta, Charlie."

She heard a few clicks of a keyboard. "It's a commercial license plate for a B-truck. Belongs to a business."

"What's the business?"

"Carrera Moving Company." A couple more clicks. "A family-owned moving company. Looks like they've been in business for about four years. They could use an update to their website. It's looking a little rough."

"Thanks, Hector. I owe you one."

"You owe me a lot more than that, Addie."

The silence that followed spoke volumes for both of them. "I know." She took a deep breath. She didn't have time for this right now, but she didn't feel right leaving it at that. "Look, I just wanted to say—"

"Save it." His voice sounded calm. "Figure this out. Get your head on straight. Then call me back." There was another pause, like Hector was trying to figure out how much to say. "Charlie and I miss you."

Harris opened her mouth, but no sounds came out. She blinked back more tears, then found her voice. But it was too late.

"I miss you too," she said. But he had already hung up.

9

CASSIE WANDERED ONCE AGAIN THROUGH THE CHICAGO HISTORY Museum. It wasn't the best place to decompress, but it was a good distraction. People milled about, murmuring to their friends and discussing the paintings in this hall. She felt the spirits in the building more than she saw them. And she felt just as lost as they did.

Tears pricked her eyes, threatening to spill down her cheeks. She felt more alone than she ever had before. David was gone, and Harris had shut her out of whatever she'd needed to do. Jason was so far away, and her family had no true understanding of what she was going through.

Cassie's chest ached, and not just from the blossoming bruise.

The boy who had gotten away hadn't meant to hurt her. But if he'd just waited and listened to what she had to say, the day could've ended differently.

Anger surged through her body, taking her by surprise. She was angry at the kid for getting one up on her. Angry at the man for escaping Harris. And angry at Harris for putting her in this position. Harris had sent her off after the kid like she was a cop. What if there had been more people waiting for her around the corner? What if the man had turned on Harris and killed her?

A gasp escaped Cassie's mouth, and a middle-aged man turned to look in her direction. Hiding her face, she shuffled into the next room without seeing where she was or what surrounded her. The thought of losing Harris had hit her like a ton of bricks. They were hardly friends. How much did Cassie really know about the detective? But Harris understood what Cassie was going through. She understood what Cassie felt.

But Cassie wasn't just angry at Harris. She was angry at David. She'd never admit it out loud, but she blamed him for leaving her. How could he do that? He knew going to that warehouse dock was a trap. He'd left Harris behind. He'd even left Cassie that letter.

Her anger intensified. Cassie's knees went weak, and she stumbled over to an empty bench. The wood was hard beneath her legs. She focused on the discomfort to distract her from Harris and David and this whole mess that had brought her to Chicago. She missed Apollo and Bear. She missed her bed. She missed Jason.

A tear slipped down her face. New Orleans had changed everything—her powers, her relationship with Jason, her understanding of what had happened to David.

And then there was the shadow. Could it have been David, or someone else? What was holding them back? It had felt as though they had wanted to tell her something, to warn her. But she couldn't decipher the words amidst all her feelings.

Cassie brushed the tear from her face. Anger continued to flicker inside of her like a flame assaulted by a gust of wind. It almost went out, only to return as bright and hot as it was before. She didn't want to be angry. But if she let go of her anger, she'd be left with the overwhelming sense of emptiness and depression.

The subtle scent of smoke caught her attention. She looked up. As the seconds ticked by, the acrid smell made her eyes prick with tears. Blinking them away, she shot to her feet, waiting to hear the alarms that told her they had to vacate the building. But no noise came, and the other patrons continued to stroll around the room unbothered.

A gentle heat caressed her skin. This was different than what she'd experienced in the jewelry store. It was more like a warm campfire on a chilly night—just enough to comfort you without searing your skin.

Cassie took a step forward, and the heat increased. The smoke burned her eyes, but she blinked away the tears. She could feel ash on her tongue. With every step, the invisible flames inched closer. Pulling off her coat, she draped it over her arm, searching the room for anything or anyone that seemed out of place.

But there was nothing. Somehow, she had wandered into the Chicago Fire exhibit. Cassie's shoulders dropped. Coming to the museum was a bad idea. She had meant for it to be relaxing and familiar. A place to clear her head. But now it was just full of smoke.

Someone brushed by her, and Cassie turned to apologize for standing in the middle of the room, lost in thought and more than a little in the way of the flow of traffic. But when she looked over her shoulder, no one was there.

Across the room, she saw another shadow pressed against the wall. This one had more form than the one from her picture, but less than the figure she'd seen in New Orleans. Her heart beat rapidly, and she could no longer smell the smoke or feel the fire kissing her skin.

Cassie pulled out her phone and took a picture of the shadow. She had accidentally left the flash on, and she winced as the light went off, causing nearly everyone in the room with her to turn in her direction.

"No flash please, ma'am," the security guard said.

"Accident." Cassie turned to flash him an apologetic grin. "Sorry. Won't happen again."

He nodded, but kept watching her. Cassie made a show of turning off her flash before facing the display across the room again. The shadow was gone. Had the light scared it away? Or had it served its purpose in garnering her attention?

Cassie picked her way across the room, trying to look natural. No one could have guessed what she had seen or experienced, but it still felt like there was a spotlight trained on her. Sure enough, when she looked over her shoulder, the security guard was still watching her. She looked away first.

The shadow had brought her over to an old map of Chicago tucked away beneath glass. The paper was browning at the edges and smudged here and there with foreign substances. It highlighted the areas of the city that had been affected by the fire. Whoever had drawn the map had used red, which seemed both appropriate and garish at the same time. It was not hard to imagine those streets burning bright, casting an orange glow over the faces of those watching their livelihoods slip away. Memories of the painting she'd seen earlier flashed through her head. She could almost hear the screams again.

Cassie leaned in closer, careful not to touch the glass. She found the river, which had protected some of the city from the devastating flames, but not all of it. And there was Kingsbury and Market Street. And just off Market Street—

The jewelry store. On the edge of the burnt district, there was no denying that the Great Chicago Fire had consumed whatever had been in its place a hundred and fifty years ago. Is that what she had been seeing? A long-forgotten victim from the late nineteenth century? Maybe the shadows had nothing to do with what had been hidden in that filing cabinet.

Maybe they had nothing to do with David's murder.

10

ZBIRAK LOVED WINTER. THE COLD RARELY BOTHERED HIM, AND THE early fall of darkness comforted him more than anything. As a child, he had been afraid of the dark, but no more. Now, he felt a quiet solace when he found himself concealed in shadow.

Of course, this was the South. December in Georgia was mild, and its citizens were more likely to encounter rain than snow. Tonight, it was a balmy sixty-three degrees—Zbirak was used to much harsher temperatures, but it was nice to travel without the encumberment of a winter jacket. He checked his watch. Just after six in the evening. A light drizzle fell across his head and shoulders. Every once in a while, a drop of water would cascade down his face. But he didn't dare move to wipe it away.

He kneeled at the base of a large tree, dressed from head to toe in black. Only his face would be visible, but the angle of the road meant no headlights would find him. He'd parked his car several miles away along the side of the road. Seemingly abandoned. No one should disturb it, but he wasn't worried either way. The car wasn't his, and he'd be rid of it by the morning.

Besides, most people who traveled the road were either lost or headed to one specific destination. Zbirak's target was in the former camp—he knew they would be traveling this road tonight, driving toward the detention center.

As promised, Francisco Aguilar had invited him to one of his restaurants for a steak dinner. Zbirak had been too polite to deny it was the best meal he'd ever had. The meat was juicy and medium rare, with plenty of seasoning. And most impressive of all was the portion. Enough to fill him up and then some. He may have eaten too much, but he regretted nothing. There was no reality in which he wasted a gift like that.

The conversation had been adequate. Aguilar was not one to mince words, spending only a few minutes on pleasantries before sending his men out of the room and getting down to business. Zbirak spent most of the remaining hour in silence, enjoying his food and soaking up every detail Aguilar could give him about the present situation.

Aguilar had hired Tony Stoll to kill Randall Sherman, the accountant who had betrayed him by going to the police. He had wanted the deed done quietly and set up to suggest that Sherman had killed himself. Stoll had followed through on neither promise. Instead, he pulled his weapon in front of a crowd, killed the accountant, and wounded the detective who had ultimately taken him down. Now, Stoll was in police custody. Dozens of witnesses had stepped forward, willing to testify in court, both for the murder of Randall Sherman and the attempted murder of the detective.

It did not take an intelligent person to see that Stoll was cornered. Aguilar had considerable power in this part of the country, but Stoll's confession to having been hired by the kingpin provided the police enough information to arrest Aguilar, even on a minor charge. And that just wouldn't do.

Aguilar had fluffed Zbirak's ego. It was something Zbirak liked about the other man—Aguilar was proud, but could admit when he was wrong. The kingpin had made a mistake in not hiring Zbirak to kill Sherman and the other detective, and he was looking to rectify the situation.

Zbirak pulled himself from the memory and looked down at his phone. Earlier in the day, he had placed a tracker on the prison transport vehicle that would take Stoll from the local prison to a detention center. Aguilar did not want to give the man a chance to breathe a word of what had transpired between them.

Zbirak's heart quickened just a fraction of a beat when he saw the illumination of headlights. A normal person would describe it as nervous excitement, but Zbirak had trained his mind and body to avoid such emotional rebellion. No, this was a prescribed dose of adrenaline, allowing his muscles to move more quickly and without fatigue.

He glanced down at his phone and frowned. The location of the tracker did not match the location of the headlights. The truck was another minute out, and these headlights looked smaller and lower to the ground, like they belonged to a car.

Who was it? Was someone lost? Had the city hired a detective to escort the truck, afraid that Aguilar would live up to his reputation and attempt to cut out the cancer before it spread? Zbirak didn't like the complication.

It was too late to change his plans now. He had already laid out the spike strip, and sure enough, the car hit the unexpected obstacle. The tires exploded like a gunshot, and even from his vantage point, he could hear someone scream.

Without wasting any time, Zbirak bolted from the shadows. The woman in the car was alone. It was not the detective who had arrested Stoll, and upon closer inspection, he realized it was simply a civilian who had ended up in the wrong place at the wrong time.

Zbirak felt a moment of pity. Unlike some of his colleagues, he did not revel in murder. It did not provide him with a sense of gratification, sexual or otherwise. He was just good at it. When one has a talent, one puts it to good use.

Still, this woman had interrupted his plans. He was at her side within seconds of her car veering off the road. When he wrenched the door open, she screamed again. Momentary relief was replaced by terror when he pulled out his hunting knife and plunged it under her chin and through her brain. A swift death was the only gift he could give her.

But his job did not end there. He placed his hand along the open wound and smeared the woman's blood across his forehead. As the lights of the truck crested the hill behind him, he rounded the vehicle and got inside the passenger seat, adjusting the woman's body to hide the wound he'd inflicted.

As expected, the truck came to a halt as soon as it spotted the car protruding halfway out of the ditch. Zbirak would have preferred it if the transport had been parked a little closer, but he'd make do with the situation. In fact, he thought wryly, the introduction of the woman in the car offered a new element to the story. The police would scratch their heads for weeks, wondering how she could possibly be connected to Stoll and Aguilar.

Zbirak watched as the passenger side door opened and a man hopped down to the asphalt. He could hear him yelling over the rumbling engine, but the words were indistinct. When the guard realized no one was answering, perhaps because they were injured, he made his way to the driver's side door.

The predictability of human nature was tedious.

Zbirak molded his current feelings of disgust until they looked more like terror. He widened his eyes. His jaw went slack with fear. He made his hands shake, and when he spoke, his voice was high and shrill and full of pain he did not feel.

"Please," he begged the man. "Please help. I don't know what happened. Sh-she's hurt. She won't w-wake up."

The man opened the door. He took in the situation, including Zbirak's bloody face and trembling lips. "It's okay. I'm an officer. I'm here to help." The guard leaned inside the car. He placed a pair of fingers at the woman's neck. "Ma'am, can you hear me?"

Zbirak was swift. He reached out his left hand as if to shake the woman awake, but grabbed the guard by his shirt collar and pulled him further into the car. With his right arm, Zbirak plunged the knife into the man's temple, burying it to the hilt. The guard slumped, and

Zbirak pulled him closer so his dead body wouldn't fall outside the car and tip off the driver behind them.

A minute or two ticked by. Curiosity got the best of the other man. In the rearview mirror, Zbirak watched as the driver opened his door and jumped down to the asphalt. The truck was left running, but that didn't matter much. Perhaps it gave the man a sense of security.

Not that it would do him much good.

Zbirak waited until the driver was halfway to the car before pushing open his door and stumbling out of the vehicle. He held a palm to his forehead and staggered around the car, toward the other man. The officer said something, but the engine was too loud to make out any words. When Zbirak looked up, he was peering down the barrel of a gun.

"I said stop where you are."

Zbirak froze. He lifted trembling hands, noticing the exact moment the other man clocked the blood on his face. The gun dropped an inch or two, but it was not enough. At this distance and this angle, a bullet would find its target.

Zbirak dropped to his knees to defuse the tension further. The impact sent a tremor through his body. His knees stung, but he felt the pain as though it were someone else's. He didn't break eye contact with the driver. He merely allowed two tears to streak down his face.

"Please," Zbirak begged. "M-my wife. Sh-she's—"

"Whoa, there, buddy." The driver dropped his weapon another few inches and took a step forward. "What happened?"

"I-I don't know." He swallowed audibly. The man took another step forward. There was eight feet between them now. Still too far. "W-we were l-lost. I should've looked at the map. B-but I thought I k-knew where we were. I should've listened to her. I should've—"

"Hey, hey, come on, now." The man's voice was gentle. He dropped his gun to his side. Took another two steps closer. He looked over at the car. "Did you hit something? Is your wife okay? Johnson'll take care of her. He's—"

But Zbirak never found out what Johnson would do. He exploded from the ground and drove his knife into someone's body for the third time that night. The driver grunted and brought up his gun, but before he could even think to squeeze the trigger, the light left his eyes, and he slumped into Zbirak's arms.

The man weighed at least two hundred and fifty pounds, but Zbirak only needed to drag him a few feet over to the car. There, he placed the body on the ground, face down, and arranged his limbs so the man's right hand was stretched out before him. Then walked back toward the truck, picking up the driver's gun where it had fallen to the ground.

There was only one thing left to do. Zbirak took a handkerchief from his pocket and wiped the blood and tears from his face. He rearranged his features into a neutral expression before grabbing the keys from the ignition and fitting the right one into the lock on the back door. A confused Tony Stoll stared back at him.

"Who the fuck are you?"

"Joseph Zbirak." He gave a little bow. "Aguilar sent me."

"To break me out?" The man's eyes lit up. "I thought for sure he'd leave me to rot."

"You've proven useful." The lie was easy. "And he doesn't like to waste his assets."

Stoll needed no further prompting. He shuffled from the back of the truck and jumped down to the road, breathing deep like a man who hadn't known freedom for twenty years. He held up his hands. "Get me outta these things."

"Ah, yes." Zbirak led the man to the other side of the truck, positioning him along the side of the road. "Wait here. I just need to grab the keys."

"Hurry up about it, will you? I gotta piss."

"Of course." Zbirak gritted his teeth. He hated impropriety. If he had his way, he'd draw out Stoll's death. But it wasn't up to him. "One moment."

Zbirak strode back toward the driver. Kneeling next to the dead body, Zbirak raised the man's gun to the right angle and aimed it at Stoll. Before Stoll understood what was happening, Zbirak squeezed the trigger. The bullet hit the other man between the eyes, and he slumped to the ground.

Four dead bodies in less than five minutes. It wasn't Zbirak's record, but he was proud of the results. He may not revel in murder, but there was no point in denying the love he had for his work.

As Zbirak made his way around the crime scene, adjusting this detail and that, wiping his prints free from the car and the truck, he found himself singing "Lovely Day" by Bill Withers under his breath. It never ceased to put a smile on his face.

With one more loose end tied up, he was closer to closing out this job and earning his paycheck. He had one more stop to make in Savannah, but it would be a fun little jaunt. Even he liked making a mess sometimes. Having an excuse to tear up someone else's home felt like the perfect way to end this lovely day.

11

THE SUN HAD ALREADY SET BY THE TIME HARRIS PULLED UP TO THE curb. Cassie piled into the car. The heat was blasting, but there was still a chill in the air. That meant Harris hadn't sat inside to make her phone calls. Where had she gone? One look at Harris's face told Cassie that was a question Harris would answer in her own time.

"I recognize the irony of this phrase," Harris started, "but you look like you've seen a ghost."

"Well, you're not far off." Cassie smoothed the worry from her face. "Another shadow person."

"David?" The detective didn't bother keeping the hope out of her voice or off her face.

"I don't think so." Cassie waited until Harris put the car in drive and pulled away from the curb before continuing. "I'm not sure the figure at the jewelry shop was David, either. Who knows if that was him in the cemetery back in New Orleans?"

"You must've had a reason to think it was him."

Cassie shrugged. "Hope? My head is spinning." She wet her lips before she continued. "The figure in the museum led me over to a map of the Great Chicago Fire. Did you know the area surrounding the jewelry store was destroyed by the fire?"

"I didn't." Harris took a moment to put on her blinker and change lanes. "But what does that have to do with David?"

"That's what I'm trying to figure out." Cassie looked out the passenger window, watching as they passed a handful of cars, not really seeing them. She was back at the store. "When I entered the shop, I felt this intense heat. Like the room was on fire, but I couldn't see any flames. Then the shadow person showed up in that picture." She turned back to Harris. "And at the museum, I could smell smoke. And another figure, or maybe the same one, showed up to point me to the map."

"But that was a hundred and fifty years ago."

"I know." Cassie shook her head and returned to the window. "And why did the first one disappear when the filing cabinet was taken?"

"We're about to find out." Harris pulled down a side street, keeping the car at the speed limit. "The van belongs to a family-owned business called Carrera Moving Company."

"Do we know anything else about it?"

"Nope." Harris pulled over and parked. When she turned to Cassie, she had a huge smile on her face. "Let's go change that."

Cassie envied Harris's endless energy and ability to walk up to a person and start chatting. Her badge must give her some of that confidence, but in the short time they'd known each other, Cassie had noticed the way Harris read people. She had the uncanny ability to get under someone's skin and force them to open up. Whatever she couldn't do one on one, she could do in an interrogation room.

But they didn't have that kind of pull here.

Carrera Moving Co. was nothing impressive, but Cassie knew how difficult it was to build a business from the ground up. The left half of the building looked more like a house than a shop, and she had a feeling the family lived where they worked. The right side of the building was a four-car garage, but much larger than anything Cassie had seen before. All the stalls were shut except one, and when she leaned to the side to get a better look, she spotted the tail end of a truck. It was dark outside, even with the porch light on, but the vehicle matched what they had seen earlier in the day.

Harris knocked on the front door, and within seconds, a plump woman with curly brown hair and heavy makeup opened the door. She was beautiful and carried with her a presence that could knock Cassie on her feet. However, Cassie could tell the woman was tired—of work, of family, of life. Her exhaustion turned to weariness as she took in the two strangers on her doorstep.

"Can I help you?" Her voice was heavily accented. If Cassie had to guess, she'd say Spanish was the woman's first language. "We book appointments over the phone."

"Actually, we're not here to book an appointment." Harris kept her voice gentle and even. This was a good lead, and they didn't want to spook the older woman. "We have some questions about your drivers."

The woman hesitated, looking Harris up and down and then casting a glance at Cassie. She must not have liked what she'd seen because she replied in rapid-fire Spanish and started to close the door. Cassie's heart dropped to her stomach.

But Harris put a hand out, stopping the door from shutting all the way. When she spoke, Cassie's brain couldn't keep up with the words. It was a moment or two before she realized Harris was speaking a foreign language. Spanish.

"Necesitamos su ayuda, por favor."

Cassie slow-blinked through the exchange, trying to absorb as much as she could. In high school and through some of college, she had studied Spanish, but she'd never been fluent. Her reading level was as basic as it came, but she could usually parse out a general meaning.

Spoken Spanish was a different story. Harris's tone of voice dropped and became softer and rounder. It had a gentle, flowing edge to it that Cassie had never heard before. It was like the detective had become a different person and Cassie was seeing her again for the first time. Did she know Harris could speak Spanish so naturally? How had it never come up before?

"Señora, por favor." Harris tried to gently hold the door open, but the woman was shaking her head and backing away into the house. "Por fa—"

When the door slammed shut, Harris hung her head. Cassie looked between the door and the detective. "I didn't really follow that."

"Yeah, sorry." Harris stared at the door as though she could will the woman to change her mind. When nothing happened, she slipped her card through the tiny gap at the bottom and stepped back onto the sidewalk. "I thought if she knew I could speak Spanish, we'd have an easier time of it. Let's just wait here for a minute in case she comes out again."

"When did you learn Spanish like that?"

"About the same time I learned English." Harris grinned when Cassie's mouth dropped open. "My mom's Puerto Rican."

"Oh."

"That gonna be a problem for you?"

Cassie blanched. "No! Of course not. I just didn't know. I'm sorry—"

"I'm joking." Harris barely contained her laughter. There was a sparkle in her eye that Cassie had missed earlier. "What are you apologizing for?"

"I, uh, don't know." Cassie added her own laugh to the mix. "For not knowing?"

Harris shrugged. "I look white. Even other Latinx people try to talk shit about who they think I am and don't realize I can understand them."

"That must be fun for you."

"The best." Harris' smile faded, but the twinkle remained. "I don't tell a lot of people. David knew." The sadness in her voice diminished the last of the spark. "But I never told anyone else. I'm not ashamed. It just makes life easier if people think I'm white."

The bitterness in Harris's voice took Cassie by surprise. "The guys at the precinct have enough to say about me being a woman. Imagine if they knew I was Latina. Or a—" She broke off suddenly, the smile back on her face. "You know what, I'll save that one for later."

Cassie didn't want to push. "What did the woman say?"

Harris cast a glance back at the house. "She said the truck had been stolen a few days ago. She didn't report it because she figured it was her son who did it."

"The kid I chased down."

"Exactly." Harris sighed. "I told her I wouldn't report him if she told me where he was. Even said I could bring the truck back. But it didn't work. She said she didn't know."

"Do you believe her?"

"I don't know." Harris turned and walked back toward the car. Thank God they had streetlamps to light the way. "She might not. Then again, she probably has a few guesses. Didn't share them with me, though. But she has my information. If he doesn't come back in a day or two, she might get desperate. We'll just have to wait it out."

"What now?"

"I see two options. We either stake out the jewelry store, or we go back through the flash drive and try to find a new lead." Harris's phone rang from her pocket. When she pulled it out, she stopped dead in her tracks. Then looked up at Cassie, worry on her face. "It's Clementine."

Cassie opened her mouth to respond, but she felt her own phone vibrating in her purse. When she pulled it out, she showed it to the detective. "Jason."

They exchanged a look. Neither one of them wanted to say what was on their mind.

Something must've happened back in Savannah.

12

CASSIE SUCKED IN A DEEP BREATH OF ICE-COLD AIR. HOLDING IT THERE, she let it burn her lungs and clear her mind. She still got nervous every time Jason called her—every time they talked was another opportunity for him to decide she was too complicated to deal with.

But she couldn't keep running away, either. "Hey."

"Hi." There was a smile in his voice. "How are you? What have you been up to?"

It felt like weeks had passed since the last time they talked. Had it really just been earlier that day? Cassie looked over at Harris, whose brow was furrowed in concentration as she talked to the Chief of Police.

"So much." She laughed. "We went to the address Adelaide found on the flash drive. It was a jewelry store. Probably a front for a money laundering scheme. Two guys showed up. Well, kind of. One was a kid. They got away, but I snapped a picture of the license plate." Cassie left out the part where the kid had laid her out on the side-walk. "It was for a moving company. Turns out the truck had been stolen, probably by this woman's son, and she won't tell us where he is."

"Wow." Jason laughed, and Cassie could tell he was still trying to take it all in. "How are you holding up?"

"Good." She shrugged her shoulders, even though he couldn't see her. "Fine. I don't know. This whole thing is a mess."

"Well, it's about to get a lot messier."

"Really? Why?"

"I may or may not have been keeping my eye out for news about the whole situation."

Cassie frowned. "Please don't feel like you have to—"

"I keep an eye out for you because I care." Pausing, he let the words sink in. Cassie blushed in response, and he continued. "But I can't say I'm not also interested. Call it professional curiosity."

"Professional?" She chuckled. "I didn't know being a museum security guard meant helping your psychic coworker solve her best friend's murder."

"I think we both know we're more than just coworkers at this point." Jason's voice held humor and heat in equal measure, and Cassie's blush deepened. "Besides, once upon a time, I was more than just a security guard."

"Right." Cassie still didn't know much about when he was an MP, but it didn't seem like the right moment to dig deeper into his past. "Well, I'm also curious. Did you find something? About David?"

"Not exactly." He sounded as though he didn't want to break the news to her. "More like something happened with Randall Sherman, the accountant."

"Something happened with him? You mean to his dead body?"

"Okay, well, not him." Now Jason sounded flustered. "His wife. Someone broke into her house."

"Why? Is she okay?"

"I don't know why. Best guess is that someone thinks she knows something."

"Aguilar must've sent his men after her. Maybe he thinks she knows something." Cassie had filled Jason in on everything. Not only did she trust him, but she knew he'd be able to help. "What happened?"

"All my information is from the news, so I'm not sure if there's more than this. We know the house was ransacked, from top to bottom. No idea if they found what they were looking for. Mrs. Sherman"—Cassie heard him flip over a piece of paper—"whose first name is Rose, is missing."

"Missing?" Goosebumps erupted across Cassie's skin. "Is she dead?"

"I have no idea." Jason sighed into the phone, and Cassie wished he was there with her, just to feel his warmth instead of the chilly Chicago air. "There was no blood at the crime scene, so they either took her away or she escaped before they got to her. She's also eight months pregnant."

"That can't be good for the baby."

"Probably not."

"Do they have any idea where she's gone?"

"If so, they're not telling the public."

Cassie scuffed her shoe against the sidewalk. "Makes sense. They don't want to tip anyone off." It was her turn to sigh into the phone. She wondered if he missed her as much as she missed him. "I wonder what she knows."

"She could be a key witness against Aguilar. I doubt she can run forever, especially at eight months pregnant."

"I wish there was something we could do."

Jason hesitated. She could feel the gears turning in his mind. "I know some people—"

"No." Cassie shook her head, and she hoped he could feel it through the phone. "You've already done so much. I don't want you to get in the middle of this."

"I want to help." His voice was quiet, and Cassie heard how genuine his words were. "I'm not the kind of person who can just stand by when I *know* I can do something."

Could she blame him? Hadn't that been her life for the last few months? With all these ghosts and visions filling her mind, she didn't feel like she could turn away from a lost soul. She'd be a hypocrite if she denied Jason the same opportunity to set things right. "Okay."

"Okay?" He sounded surprised. "Are you sure?"

"I'm sure." She smiled, and she knew he could hear it in her voice. "I appreciate the help. Adelaide will, too. If things don't work out here in Chicago, maybe we'll have a new lead to come home to. Just do me a favor?"

"Anything."

Cassie's heart fluttered at his response. It took her a second to refocus and get back on track. "Please be careful. Aguilar is dangerous. If he sees you poking around, he might send someone after you too. And I can't—" Cassie's voice broke, and she had to clear her throat before she could talk again. "I've already lost one person I care about. I can't lose another."

"I know." Jason's voice was hushed. Gentle. "I promise. I'll just talk to a few people and see if I can dig anything up. I'll be discreet."

"Thank you."

"And Cassie?"

"Yeah?"

"You be careful, too, okay? I don't want to lose you either."

Cassie smiled, despite their grave proclamations. "I promise."

As Cassie hung up, Harris stood with her hands shoved in her pockets, far enough away to give her some privacy. Cassie made a show of putting the phone back in her purse, and Harris gestured for her to come closer.

"Come on, I'm freezing." Harris' shoulders were hiked up to her ears. "Let's get back to the car."

Cassie nodded and crossed the street with the detective. When they reached the other side, she cast a glance at Harris. "I'll tell you about mine if you tell me about yours."

Harris didn't laugh. "Tony Stoll is dead."

Cassie stumbled to a stop, and when Harris didn't slow down, she had to jog to catch back up. "The guy who killed Sherman? The guy who almost killed you?"

"He didn't almost kill me." But Harris rubbed her arm where the man had shot her. "But yeah, him."

"How? What happened?"

"He was headed to a detention center before his trial. Clementine was gonna send a few guys his way in a couple days, see if she could get him to talk."

"Would he have talked?"

"Oh yeah." Harris shook her head. "And that's probably why he was killed."

Cassie's voice came out as a whisper. "How'd he die?"

"They're not sure. Still trying to put the pieces together. But Stoll died along with the two guards transporting him. Plus a woman who might've just been in the wrong place at the wrong time."

"A woman?" Cassie's focus snapped back to attention. "Who? Do you know her identity?"

"Elise Porter, I think." Harris caught Cassie's concern. "Why? What do you know?"

"Nothing. Well, not about this."

"I told you mine," Harris said. "Your turn."

"Jason's been keeping an eye on the news."

"Uh oh."

"It's fine. He's smart."

"Let's hope so." Harris didn't sound convinced.

Cassie tried not to raise her hackles in his defense. "Rose Sherman, Randall's wife, is missing. Her house was ransacked."

It was Harris's turn to stop in her tracks. "Kidnapped?"

Cassie kept walking, and it only took a few strides for Harris to catch up again. "He doesn't know. The news isn't sharing a ton of information. But there was no blood. Maybe she escaped. But she's eight months pregnant. It's gonna be hard for her to stay ahead of Aguilar."

"You got that right." Harris sounded distant. "I don't get it."

"What?"

Finally reaching the car, Harris hit the button to unlock it. They climbed inside, neither talking until the engine was running and the heat was blasting out of every single vent. Harris stared down at her hands while she answered. "I thought Clementine was telling me about Stoll out of professional courtesy."

"You don't think she did?"

Harris looked up. "She asked me where I was, what I was up to, so I told her I was in Chicago. Then she told me about Stoll."

"Does she think you have something to do with it?"

"I wouldn't be surprised if the thought crossed her mind. He did shoot me, after all."

"Just a graze," Cassie retorted.

Harris smiled, but it didn't reach her eyes. "Why didn't she tell me about Rose Sherman?"

"There's no world in which she didn't already know, is there?"

"None." Harris shook her head and put the car in gear. "Seems like she doesn't want me to know any more than I have to." Easing off the brakes, she checked her side mirror. "We'd solve this much faster if we all worked together."

Cassie didn't disagree, but kept her mouth shut as Harris entered the flow of traffic. Was Clementine just following protocol by keeping a suspended officer out of the loop about her former case? Or was she being cautious because she thought Harris was about to go off the deep end?

Cassie wished she knew the answer.

13

CASSIE OPENED THE DOOR TO THEIR HOTEL ROOM AND SCRUNCHED HER nose at the overly powerful scent of lavender and bleach. She popped her head into the bathroom and flicked the light switch. The bathtub gleamed. Maybe it didn't smell the best, but at least everything was clean.

"Is it up to your standards?" Harris asked. She was still standing in the hallway, waiting for Cassie to keep moving.

"Oh, sorry." Cassie shuffled forward and turned on a couple of lights. She pointed between the two beds. "Do you have a preference?"

"Closest to the door."

"Got it." Cassie tossed her duffle bag down on the second bed. "Is that so if something happens, you can escape faster and leave me behind to fend for myself?"

Harris didn't bother looking up. "It's so if someone breaks into the room, they'll attack me first, and I can take care of them before they ever get to you."

Cassie froze. That was a very real possibility now, wasn't it? "Oh."

Harris laughed. "Relax, it's not going to happen." She tossed a backpack onto the bed and then flopped down next to it, shimmying up toward the pillow. "Bed's not half bad. Could be worse."

"We could've gotten a motel—"

"Nah, too far out of town. I wanted to stay close." Harris sat up and undid the zipper on the larger section of the backpack. "Plus, I wanted to use some points. Did you know they never expire? Got this room for free."

"Really?" Cassie stood up a little taller. "Good to know."

"Just don't go breaking anything."

"I wouldn't—"

"Joking." Harris tossed Cassie a look that told her she needed to lighten up. Then she held up her computer. "You ready for this?"

"Ready for what?"

"The flash drive."

The weight settled back onto Cassie's shoulders. She wasn't sure what to expect from this little piece of technology. The last person to hold it in their hands, besides Harris, was a dead man. Randall Sherman had met an untimely end because of what was inside. Not to mention, his coming forward with this information was also the reason David was dead. Then there was the issue of Harris having never turned it in to the Chief in the first place.

A little knot of dread settled in Cassie's stomach, but she looked up at Harris and gave her a nod anyway.

"Right." The detective plugged the flash drive into her computer and waited for the window to open. "There are nine folders. They all have miscellaneous names. Names are random or code for something only Sherman knew."

"Why would he want to give David a flash drive he couldn't even read?"

"My best guess is that Sherman wanted to make sure David still needed him after handing over the flash drive. He trusted David, but Sherman also didn't want David to dump him as soon as he got it."

Cassie turned back to the folders. There were a few names on there: *Caine* and *Mary* and *Hermes*. But there were other random words too. Like *Blue, Push,* and *Clean.*

"Okay, which ones have you figured out?" Cassie asked.

Harris double clicked on the folder that read *Caine*. "This is where I found the address."

Cassie leaned closer. The folder was full of excel spreadsheets. Each of these had a codename. Harris clicked on the first one. "I see a bunch of dates and some dollar amounts."

"Transaction dates and amounts. It's essentially an invoice." She scrolled down. "See? This one takes place on the date David died. I haven't matched up the other dates yet, but I think each of them represents another murder."

"How can you know—" Cassie paused. "Caine." She rolled her eyes. "The first murderer."

Harris nodded her head, her eyes alight with excitement. "Exactly. I think each spreadsheet represents a killer for hire. Aguilar will have different people on his roster, all with different specialties. He doesn't want to get his hands dirty, so he'll put as many people between him and these guys as possible."

"So, if we link Aguilar to a few of these murders, we can send him to prison?"

"Since Sherman's dead, I doubt it." Harris didn't sound nearly as crestfallen as Cassie felt. "It's likely he was the only one who had the master key. And it's possible he didn't even write that down. Look here." She pointed to the corner of the spreadsheet. "Each assassin has their own codename. This one is Zephyr."

"That's two for two on Greek names."

"I'm not sure that's a pattern," Harris said. "It's going to be as random and difficult as possible. I bet this guy's real name isn't written down anywhere. It's just a way to remember who's who for the sake of accounting."

Cassie sat up. "What about the wife? Rose, I mean. Could she know anything? Have the master key?"

"It's possible. We need to figure out where she is. That's a lot harder to do this far from Savannah, though."

"Jason's working on it." When Cassie saw Harris's eyebrows lift in question, she hurried on. "He knows people, and he knows how to be discreet. He might find a lead."

Harris turned back to the computer. "Well, until then, this is what we have to work with."

"Where did you get the address?"

Harris closed the spreadsheet and returned to the folder labeled *Caine*. She clicked on another spreadsheet simply labeled *X*. "It's full of addresses. Dozens of them." Harris scrolled and stopped on one. "Each one has letters next to it. This one had a *Z*. I put two and two together."

"As in, Zephyr might be the one to frequent the location?"

"Exactly."

Harris looked proud, but Cassie was doubtful. That was a lot of jumps to make about something they still knew little about. Sure, it all made sense, but proving this in a court of law? That'd be impossible without further evidence.

"Okay." Cassie rubbed a finger against her temple. "Let's say this all makes sense. Where do we go from there?"

"The other locations are either in California or New York. Chicago was the closest, which is why I chose that one, and I don't think we're done here yet."

"I realize I don't need to explain the law to you," Cassie said, as gently as she could, "but if we're crossing state borders, we should turn this over to the FBI." Her mind flickered to Agent Viotto. Charlotte felt like a lifetime ago, but she still had his number. He would help Cassie, she was sure of it. "They have a lot more manpower than we do."

"This is personal." Harris caught Cassie's concerned look and threw up a pair of hands. "Look, you're right. It's stupid to dig into this on our own. But something doesn't sit right with me, and I want to know what's going on before it's all taken away from me. The FBI isn't going to care about why David didn't tell me he was meeting the witness on his own. I'll never know the answer if I don't do this myself."

"What if we're wasting time?" Cassie's voice shook, and it took all her will to get it under control. "What if David's killer gets away because we kept this all to ourselves?"

"I won't let that happen."

"You don't have control over that."

Harris took a deep breath. "You're right. I don't. Look, let's make a deal, okay? Let's follow through on a couple of these leads. If we keep hitting dead ends, we stop bashing our skulls against the wall and hand this over to someone who can do something about it."

"And if we do actually find something? You and I can't take down Aguilar on our own."

"If we find something, we hand it over to Clementine."

"Deal," Cassie relented. "What's next?"

Harris closed out of the addresses and backed out of the *Caine* folder. "Pick another one."

"Really? Just like that?"

"Why not? We've got nothing to lose."

Cassie skimmed the folders. A few went together, like *Caine* and *Mary*. And there was the one labeled *Hermes* that could've gone with *Zephyr*. Then there were plain ones like *Blue*. "That one." Cassie pointed to it.

Harris double-clicked on the folder. "All right, just a single spreadsheet in here. Looks like each section has an ID number. Then dates and rows of amounts."

Cassie leaned closer to get a better look. "Money paid or money owed?"

"Looks like paid, though some of them have subtractions."

"What do you think the numbers are for?"

"Not sure. Could represent people or companies. Maybe they're random, or maybe they're tied to something speci—" Harris froze.

Cassie looked from Harris to the computer and back again. "What is it?"

Harris pointed a finger at the screen. There was a line with a four-digit number, no date, and a zero in the space for the dollar amount. "That's my badge number."

Cassie looked again. "Eight-four-three-two. You're sure?"

"Of course I'm sure."

"I mean, are you sure that's supposed to be your badge number? It could be anything."

"The folder is labeled *Blue*."

"Like the boys in blue." Cassie sat up straight. "These are cops Aguilar tried to pay off?"

"Maybe." She shook her head. "He never got to me, but does this mean I was on his shortlist?"

The knot in Cassie's stomach got tighter. "What's David's number?"

"Eight-one-seven-seven."

"Search it."

"You can't be serious."

Cassie looked her dead in the eyes. There was a reason David didn't want her to investigate his death, and she needed to know why. "Search it."

Harris's fingers paused over the keyboard, but as she took a deep breath, she pressed each number in turn. When she hit enter, they both held their breath.

There was one result.

Harris scrolled to the match. It was David's badge number, all right. And a list of dozens of dates. But instead of monetary payments, it just said DEBT in capital letters. Cassie looked up at Harris, wanting the other woman to have some sort of explanation for this. Wanting her to tell Cassie it wasn't true.

Instead, Harris slammed the laptop shut. "That's enough of that for tonight."

"Adelaide—"

"There's another explanation."

"What is it? Your badge number is on there. His is on there. Do you know anyone else's?"

"Not tonight. Not now. I need to think."

"Adelaide—"

Harris turned to Cassie with such ferocity in her eyes, Cassie sat back in her chair. It looked like Harris was tempering her voice, but a fury lurked just under the surface. She sounded monotone. Dead. "Not tonight. Please. I have some things to think about. To get straight in my head. We can talk about it in the morning."

Cassie didn't have the heart—or the courage—to argue.

14

BY THE TIME THEY WOKE UP IN THE MORNING, HARRIS WAS BACK TO HER normal self. Cassie waited for her to bring up what they had discovered the night before, but the detective avoided the topic like the plague. But she did mention she'd gotten a new idea in the middle of the night.

"Someone owned the jewelry shop. They had to lease that building, right? We should go to City Hall and see if we can find any information about it."

Cassie didn't want to argue. She was reeling from the information, too. As much as she tried to avoid thinking about it, she kept coming to the same conclusion: It looked like David had taken money from Aguilar over several years.

But David was a good cop. A good *person*. He'd never take money, and if he did, there had to be a compelling reason. But Cassie also couldn't stop thinking about David's letter. About how he hadn't wanted them to look into his death. To just let it go. She felt so naïve for thinking she knew better.

With that thought in mind, Cassie joined Harris in going to City Hall. The drive was painfully silent, so Cassie looked up some information on the building to pass the time.

Construction had begun in 1909, and city employees occupied its halls in 1912. Over the years, renovations had taken place, and in 2001, they installed a roof garden. The pictures were breathtaking. However, it was nothing compared to the real thing.

As Harris hurried through the doors, Cassie stopped to gaze at the massive structure. At the time, critics had called it pretentious, and while she didn't disagree, the building certainly made an impact. It had all the grandeur of classical architecture, with purely decorative Corinthian columns adorning the outside standing at a whopping seventy-five feet tall. From here, she couldn't see much detail of the relief sculptures, but she knew they were there.

Cassie hurried inside, met by an impatient Harris. "What were you doing?"

Cassie couldn't answer. The interior of the building was just as glorious. High vaulted ceilings and floors that gleamed with a mirror finish. It was like stepping back in time. Architecture was far from her specialty, and yet Cassie couldn't help but appreciate such classic beauty.

What would it have been like to work here back when it was brand new? There'd be fewer ghosts, at least. Not that they were paying her much mind. The few who lingered in the grand entrance seemed stuck in a time loop, unable to escape the daily grind that had consumed them when they were alive. She felt sorry for them, but they added to the atmosphere of the building.

Not that anyone else could see them like she could.

"Cassie." Harris was holding open the doors of an elevator. Two other people were already inside. "Come on."

With an apologetic grimace, Cassie slipped inside the elevator and watched as Harris punched the number for the first floor. In silence, the four of them rose to the next level, where only Cassie and Harris got off. Cassie wanted to see the rest of the building, but Harris was already marching down the hall, toward her destination.

It turned out they weren't in City Hall, but the other half of the building that housed the Cook County Clerk's Office, specifically the Recordings Division. Harris knew exactly where to go, and after pausing briefly at the threshold of one of the rooms, she walked inside and up to the front desk.

On the other side sat a man who looked like he belonged in a basement next to a boiler, sipping on black coffee and rummaging through garbage and loose papers to fulfill his requests. He had pale skin and gray eyes—the effect enough to make Cassie pause, wondering if he was actually alive—though they were hidden behind large bottle-cap glasses. His mousy brown hair was greasy and flecked with silver. Even so, Cassie could see his strong jaw and high cheekbones. He'd definitely turn some heads, if only he'd take a look in the mirror once in a while.

"Can I help you?" he asked, not bothering to look up.

"I hope so, sir." Harris's voice was full of charm. Cassie had never heard her so amiable. "I'm looking for information on a public building. I'd like to know who owns it, so I can speak to them about possibly purchasing it."

They had not discussed any of this on the way in, and Cassie suddenly felt at a loss for what to do. Silence seemed to be the best solution. She plastered a smile on her face for good measure.

The man looked up, taking in Harris with complete disinterest. He pulled a packet of papers from his desk and slapped them on the counter. "Fill out the information here. We'll send you a copy of the documents within a week, if they're available."

"Ah." Harris's face fell. "Is there an expedite fee? I'd be happy to pay."

That caught the man's attention. For the first time, he seemed to take Harris in, from her high ponytail to her long jacket and that smile that looked as dangerous as it did disarming. His eyes shifted, and he spotted Cassie, who didn't look like she belonged with the badass in front of him. Still, she stood a bit taller under his gaze.

"No expedite fee. It's a week or nothing."

Cassie felt a tingle in the back of her neck. The man was lying, but she wasn't sure why. Harris didn't look like a cop, but then again, this *wasn't* some boiler room-turned-office, which meant the guy behind the desk would have to be more discerning about who he let cut in line. Someone else would need to vouch for them to make sure they weren't working with the police. Someone like—

"Jonesy sent us." As soon as the name popped into her head, she blurted it out. She had no idea who the hell Jonesy was, but the guy behind the desk seemed to recognize the name. "He said you'd help us."

"He sent you, huh?"

"Yep." Cassie forced herself to look nonchalant, almost bored. Harris kept the smile plastered to her face, but when she glanced at Cassie, there were questions in her eyes. "So? What do you say?"

The guy huffed and leaned back in his chair. "It's a hundred dollars to get it by the end of the day."

Harris swooped in. "Two hundred and you work on it now."

The man's eyes twinkled. He opened his mouth. "What about—"

"No." Harris's congenial demeanor was gone. "Two hundred is far more than you expected to make today. Don't be greedy."

The man seemed to take her pushback in stride. "A hundred up front."

Harris slipped a hand from her pocket and held it out for the man to shake. He did so with a smile on his face. "What information do you need from me?" she asked.

"We'll start with the address."

Cassie settled into a chair as Harris gave the man the address of the jewelry store, which he typed into the computer. Harris had told her the owner was listed as a John Richards, but when the detective had tried to dig deeper, she found that no such person existed. She needed the city's records.

"Limitless Holdings," the man said.

"I'm going to need a little more than that, uh—"

"Gerry."

"Gerry." Harris flashed him a million-watt smile. "Owners, addresses, phone numbers if you've got them."

Gerry didn't seem deterred by the fact that Harris was letting him off easy. In fact, he seemed to thrive on the contention. "Limitless Holdings is owned by John Richards."

"Fake name. Keep looking."

Gerry tapped away on his keyboard. "John Richards is also part owner of King Richard & Co."

"Who owns it with him?"

"Ah, let's see." He pushed his glasses up his nose. "Richard Johnson. Ha. I see what he did there."

"Very clever." Harris's tone indicated she thought it was anything but. "I doubt that's a real name, either. Keep looking."

"The addresses match, and when I search for that property—yes, it belongs to a different company. Annex, LLC."

"Owner?"

"None listed." He held up a finger before Harris could interrupt. "But there is a lawyer listed. A Mr. Don A. Reed. A quick search and" —he paused to hit enter and watch the page load—"seems like we hit the real deal. He's got an office not far from here."

"Perfect." She nodded toward the computer. "Print that out for me, will you?"

"Ah." The man looked nervous for the first time. "Paper trail."

"I could always take a picture of your screen." Harris held up her phone, clearly aiming it at him. "Would that be better?"

Gerry's hand shot up, hiding his face from the camera. "I'll print it out."

"Wonderful!" Harris's chipper voice laced with insincerity.

Gerry hit a button on his keyboard, and the printer behind him started chugging away. He turned away from Harris, as though he didn't trust her not to sneak a picture of him after all. When the papers had slid into the tray, he grabbed them and held them out for the detective.

Harris slipped her hand from her pocket where it had been resting, shaking his hand with her own while she took the papers in the other. "It was a pleasure, Gerry. You have a nice day."

The man didn't bother responding. Even the two hundred dollars didn't seem enough to put him at ease over the idea of possibly seeing the paperwork traced back to him. But when Cassie cast one last glance over her shoulders on the way out, he had already returned to work as though nothing had happened within the last fifteen minutes.

Harris was nearly skipping to the elevator, like she hadn't just paid off a city official to give her information that should've taken a week through the proper channels. Cassie wasn't sure what to make of the situation. She was grateful they had a new lead, but if any of this came to light in court, it could cost them a conviction.

The elevators closed, and Harris turned to Cassie. "Jonesy, huh? Where'd you get that name?"

Cassie tapped the side of her head. "I had a tingle."

"A tingle?"

She shrugged. "Don't know what else to call it. Had a tingle in the back of my head. Name just sort of came to me. I said it. It worked."

Harris was trying not to laugh and doing a poor job of it. "Well, let me know if you tingle again. It's a very useful superpower."

15

CASSIE AND THE DETECTIVE SUCKED IN A SHARP GASP AS THE ICY BREEZE assaulted them. They'd only been inside for half an hour—long enough for their body temperatures to return to normal. It made going back outside even worse.

"Reed's office is a couple of blocks away." Harris pulled her jacket up around her chin. "Let's walk."

Cassie couldn't think of a good reason to walk instead of drive, but she didn't argue. She had more important matters on her mind. "About last night—"

"Let's tackle one thing at a time."

Cassie bit down on her frustration, not wanting to push the subject. It looked as though David had taken money from Aguilar, but there had to be another reason Harris had shut her out. Why couldn't her psychic abilities give her the answers she wanted to know?

They arrived at Reed's office building before she could think of another way to get Harris to open up. The two-story structure carried all the age and none of the grandeur of City Hall. The bricks were faded and dirty with a hundred years of city life. There were no ornamental figures across the façade. Even the old-fashioned marquee that bore the words *Don A. Reed, Attorney at Law* looked dilapidated. This wasn't an aesthetic choice to uphold the vintage atmosphere of the building—it had been kept in place out of sheer laziness.

Harris pulled open the door and stepped inside. Cassie followed, unimpressed with the way the building had been kept up over the years. An ornate rug adorned the hallway and the stairs leading up and to the right. At one point, it had been beautiful, but now it was more mud than fabric. The wood paneling along the walls was cracked and dull. The banister—which must have once gleamed in the light of the now cobweb-infested chandelier—was rubbed raw from years of use. If someone had had the heart to restore it a decade or so ago, it might've been salvaged. Now it was too late.

A man standing in the hallway looked up as they entered. He wore the navy-blue jumpsuit of a janitor and filled out every inch of it. He wasn't tall, but stout with arms that bulged against the seams of his uniform. The tattoo along his neck was partially hidden by his collar and shoulder-length gray hair. His beady black eyes followed their every movement, even while he rinsed his mop and slopped it against the floor, spreading more dirt than he cleaned up. Cassie could smell the putrid water from the door.

If Harris was bothered by his presence, she didn't let it show. She turned to the directory just inside the door. All of the metal plaques for other businesses had been removed or scratched out. The only one left read *Don A. Reed, Attorney at Law*. On the second floor in room 204.

The stairs creaked with every step. Even though Reed's office was at the end of the hall, she imagined he could hear them coming. On the landing, the floorboards moaned under their weight. The putrid scent of the mop water accompanied them, and Cassie wondered if the man downstairs washed the floor with it to keep normal clientele out of the building.

The door to room 204 was open. Harris stepped inside, but Cassie hovered at the entrance. This area was a degree or two hotter, and she couldn't tell if it was from the heating system or something else. Either way, it was empty save for an unoccupied desk. She spotted another door on the opposite side of the room. It was closed, but sounds radiated from within.

Harris closed the distance and rapped her knuckles twice on the door. No one answered, even though they could hear someone on the other side. Harris knocked again. A man with a raspy voice shouted, "Go away!"

Harris didn't listen. Tossing a look over her shoulder, the detective shrugged at Cassie and opened the door uninvited. Cassie scrambled after her, noting the temperature of the room rising another degree. But any thoughts of supernatural occurrences went out the window when she got a glimpse of the room.

Folders were strewn about the place. Stacked on tables, chairs, the floor. The room smelled like old deli meat and cigars. The air was stale and oppressive. Cassie suppressed a cough, but Harris wasn't so lucky. She erupted into a fit, waving her hand in front of her face as though it would clear the room of the smell. The man behind the desk didn't even bother looking up.

"Get out," he said. "No appointments today."

Don A. Reed was both nothing like Cassie had pictured and exactly who she thought he would be. Short, squat, and balding, he wore large glasses and held an unlit cigar between his teeth. He wore a white tank top and suspenders, which at least indicated he was also wearing pants, but his button-down shirt was tossed over a peg on the coat rack, along with a beat-up tan and brown fedora. He'd be perfectly cast in a mobster movie, and certainly not as one of the good guys.

"I just have a couple questions for you," Harris began.

Reed looked up at the sound of Harris's voice and his eyes went wide at the sight of them. Cassie couldn't decide if it was because they were women or because he had never expected two people who looked like them to show up at his door. But as soon as the surprise came, it dissipated.

"Don't have time." He gestured to the paperwork around him. Cassie spotted at least three empty coffee cups, and one of them had started growing mold. "Don't you see I'm busy here?"

"It'll only take a minute." Harris's voice was bubbly, but firm. Tossing a stack of folders onto the floor, she sat down in a chair opposite him. "I have a business proposition for you."

Cassie followed Harris's lead, grabbing a pile of folders from the other chair and dropping them to the floor. The chair was deep red, made darker by years of dirt and sweat and—oh God, was that blood? Cassie perched herself on the edge of the seat, doing her best to touch as little of the fabric as possible. She held her fist over her mouth to hide her gagging.

When she looked up again, Reed was staring at her. Lowering her fist, she smiled, looking away. The stack of folders on the edge of his desk between them were piled so high, she could just make out his eyes over the top. Some of them appeared to have been left in the rain or dumped into a pot of coffee.

She noticed a tab in her direction about halfway down the stack. There was no mistaking the word printed in blue ink and careful handwriting that didn't match his persona. It said *Annex*. If he tried to deny he was associated with the company, she had proof right in front of her.

Cassie hugged her purse to her chest and slipped her phone out of the front pocket. Maybe Jason could find more information on this guy. If the file folders were any indication, he probably had his hand in a lot of businesses—and may have slipped up somewhere.

"What are you doing?" Reed's rough voice jolted Cassie in her seat. He was staring right at her. "Put your phone away."

Cassie didn't bother trying to hide it. "I just wanted to take notes."

"No notes." The man was going red in the face. "No phones. Leave. Before I make you leave."

Harris pinched her lips together, but Cassie couldn't tell who the detective was more annoyed with. Reed's threat was likely empty, but they didn't want to rock the boat so soon. Harris could've taken Reed on her own, but the man downstairs was another story. He'd give her a proper fight—plus, they had no idea who else was in the building.

"It's fine," Harris said, motioning for Cassie to put her phone away. "No need to take notes."

Cassie shrugged, swiping up on her device to get to the camera. "As long as you're sure," she said, making a show of holding up her phone so he could track its movements as she went to place it back inside her purse.

Her breath caught as she fought to remember if she'd left her ringer on.

The shutter snapped silently, and she held back a sigh of relief. The photo was a little blurry, but clear enough to see what he looked like. As she pretended to fumble to put it back in her purse, she typed out a message to Jason: *Don Reed. Lawyer. Annex.* Then attached the picture. She couldn't risk waiting to see if the text sent, so she slipped it back inside her purse and sat up straighter, all smiles.

"What do you want?" Reed snapped, staring at Harris.

"I buy and sell properties all over the United States, and I'm interested in a certain jewelry store in your possession. I want to turn it into a high-end shop for luxury furs, and I was hoping we could come to an arrangement."

"I don't own any jewelry stores. You've wasted your time." He returned to the papers on his desk. "And mine."

"Annex, LLC?" Harris leaned forward, her voice sweet as honey. "You're listed as the primary contact."

"I don't own—"

"I know." Harris' smile broadened. "I want to know who your employer is. I want to strike a deal with him—or her."

"Nice try, lady. We're not interested."

"You haven't even heard my proposal."

"I said we're not interested." Reed looked up, and for the first time, Cassie sensed danger. This man might not be physically imposing, but the way he held himself told her he wasn't afraid of much. "Leave."

"Why don't you just tell me the name of—"

Reed bristled. "I said—"

"Let's go." Cassie stood up, ignoring the sharp look Harris gave her. "We don't need him. We have plenty of other clients."

"Listen to your friend, lady," Reed growled. "You'll find nothing here."

Harris rose from her chair. Cassie leaned over the stack of papers and stuck her hand in the man's face, waiting for him to shake it. She was grateful she wasn't wearing a low-cut top—not that it stopped him from looking—but regretted the gesture as soon as his hand touched hers. She would've been able to ignore the grease clinging to his skin, but as soon as their fingers made contact, a searing heat shot up her arm and nearly made her knees buckle.

Cassie yelped and yanked her hand back, knocking over the pile of folders on the desk. "I'm so sorry," she stuttered, while Reed yelled at her, and Harris yelled at him. Cassie dropped to her knees and started shuffling papers back into their folders and tossing them onto the desk one at a time. But when she got to the one labeled *Annex*, Cassie shoved it in her purse, gathered the remaining folders, and dropped them in front of Reed with an apologetic smile. "I'm so, so sorry."

"Get out!" He was practically jumping up and down now. "Get out. Get out."

Harris emerged from the room with her head held high, but Cassie kept her eyes on the ground. She didn't want to risk Reed getting a sense that she'd taken something from him. They needed to get out of the building as soon as possible.

Harris came to a halt at the top of the stairs and whirled around, glaring at Cassie. Her teeth were clenched so tightly, her words came out like a hiss. "What the hell?"

Cassie didn't bother answering. She couldn't risk anyone over-hearing, and she couldn't trust the janitor to not report their conversation to Reed.

Grabbing the detective's hand, she dragged her out the front door, ignoring the man still mopping the floor with dirty water. It wasn't until they were back inside the car that Cassie produced the folder and held it up for Harris to read.

The detective's broad grin told Cassie that, despite her better judgment, she'd made the right call.

16

Zbirak hadn't been back to this property in eighteen months. It was one of his favorites. A cream-colored duplex with a large wrap-around porch and a small backyard. He used to rent out the other side to a young couple, but as soon as the wife got pregnant, they moved to a larger house. He didn't need the money, but it had been nice knowing someone was making use of half the house. There had been far fewer attempted break-ins at that time.

There wasn't much to steal in his half, however. All his most important belongings—his guns, his passports, his cash—were tucked away where only he could get to them.

Still, he had upgraded his alarm system and hadn't had any trouble since. It only took one unlucky bastard getting caught red-handed for the word to travel. The rest of them would stay away. Everyone loved an easy target, and Zbirak was anything but.

He shrugged his duffel bag up higher on his shoulder and pulled out his set of keys. Snow still covered the sidewalk and porch steps, and he was happy to see there weren't any footprints in the fresh powder. At least, no human prints.

Vermin were an issue. He didn't leave food here, but mice, squirrels, and raccoons liked the insulated walls and the quiet of an empty house. Every three months, he sent around a guy to check his attic. It was the only other person he had given the code to, but it was worth it to keep rodents from chewing on his wires.

It took him a few seconds to find the right key, and he took that time to listen for anyone approaching him from behind. Some might think he was paranoid, but having as many enemies as he did, he benefited from staying vigilant.

As soon as he fit the key into the door's lock and twisted it to the right, a soft beeping emanated from the panel just inside the entrance. He kept a tally of the beeps in his head. He had purposely shortened the timer in case any burglars managed to get past his first line of defense.

Dropping his duffle on the front porch, Zbirak waited until thirty seconds had passed before popping open the panel on the alarm system and typing in an eight-digit code. He pressed enter, and repeated the code one more time, changing the final number from an eight to a three. Upon hitting enter one more time, he closed the panel and turned toward his home, ears pricked to catch any unusual sounds.

Zbirak pulled his gun and stalked forward, sweeping left to right as he crossed the small living room. There was a sofa along one wall and a moderately sized television across from it. A few bookcases guarded the entrance to the kitchen, also empty. He peered out the back windows. At this point in the year, the snow wouldn't melt until Spring. He was happy to see it was smooth and even, except for a few spots with animal tracks.

Retracing his steps, Zbirak swung back around and headed for the stairs. He stayed along the outside, avoiding the one in the middle that creaked no matter where you stood. When he reached the landing, he checked the bathroom, then made his way to the two bedrooms. Only one had a bed, and it was this one he checked first, careful to avoid stepping on the tripwire he had placed at the entrance.

Lastly, Zbirak pulled down the ladder to the attic, pausing to listen for scrambling. After a few seconds, he popped his head through the door for a visual confirmation. There were dozens of different sized boxes littered across the floor. But if anyone tried opening them, they'd be in for a nasty surprise.

Satisfied that his house had remained untouched, Zbirak lowered himself back down the ladder, closed the attic, and headed downstairs. He grabbed his duffel and took one last deep breath of the chilly outside air before closing the front door. Then he shut all the curtains on the first floor and got to work.

After spending most of the night on the road, he was happy to stretch out. He'd taken a few hours to sleep while pulled over along the shoulder, but it hadn't been ideal. To loosen up his stiff body and get more blood pumping to his brain, he did a few calisthenic exercises in his living room. When he was satisfied, he flipped on the TV and pulled out his arsenal.

Zbirak wasn't a religious person, but he believed the universe operated outside of his own desires. In other words, it would align itself to its own interests, regardless of his needs. As a result, he made sure not to take any more risks than necessary. That's why checking his weapons after every job was so important to him.

Placing a towel on the floor, Zbirak pulled out the knife he'd used to murder the woman and the cops, and cleaned off every spot of blood. Then he moved on to his pistol, disassembling it and cleaning each part with precision. He let his mind wander to the reporter on the television, a large Black man in a gray suit and navy tie. As the man read the latest report, a frown creased his face.

"Boyd Weathers here, reporting for ABC 7 in Chicago. Adriana King, twenty-three, was killed early this morning after a bullet penetrated the bedroom window of her apartment on Chicago's South Side. Those who knew her described her as a good friend and excellent mother. Her son, Andre, is four years old."

Zbirak shook his head. What a waste. He wondered if the woman he had killed the night before had been a mother. She hadn't been wearing a wedding ring, though that didn't tell him much. Then again, her death hadn't been an accident like Adriana King's. She'd simply been in the wrong place at the wrong time.

Rather, she had been in the right place at the right time—for him. It would be enough of a curveball for the police. Now that he was no longer in Savannah, he was sure they wouldn't be able to trace him to Chicago. This was one of his safest locations. And it was where he'd needed to go next.

Zbirak had been thorough when he had gone through Rose Sherman's house. He was sure to make it look like it had been ransacked, but he'd only pulled one piece of evidence from her home. He took it out of his bag and smoothed it onto the coffee table as he shifted to perch on the edge of the couch.

It was a boarding pass, left behind in a moment of panic and confusion. He felt another wave of annoyance at Pisano for tipping her off. She'd left in a hurry, barely packing anything before abandoning her house and making a run for it. Normally, Zbirak would've stayed in town and done his research—what family did she trust most? Where would she be more likely to go? But he hadn't needed to. The boarding pass was enough.

It was for a flight to O'Hare International Airport. Typically, that wouldn't be too much cause for celebration. Chicago was a large city, and even someone like Mrs. Sherman would've been able to disappear if she was clever enough. But her mistake had been scribbling down a phone number on the edge of the pass. Even if the ticket had been fake, left behind on purpose and meant to throw him off her scent, he doubted the phone number served the same purpose. And it started with a Chicago area code.

Zbirak pulled out his laptop and typed the phone number into a program on his computer. Sure enough, when the name populated the results field, a small smile spread over his face.

Robert Sherman.

Zbirak opened an incognito window in his browser and typed in the name, the number, and the word *Chicago*. The results were easy to find. Bob Sherman only had one social media profile—Facebook. His wife, on the other hand, had accounts on Facebook, Twitter, and Instagram. She even had a burgeoning YouTube channel where she taught people how to crochet dolls for their friends and family.

Melissa was a pre-school teacher, and Bob an investment banker. They had one child, little Georgie, and made a modest income. But the internet could only tell Zbirak so much. He wanted to know Bob's schedule, his habits and mannerisms, his greatest fears and deepest desires.

Zbirak hooked his cell phone to the computer and changed phone numbers, mimicking a toll-free automated text service. Then he sent a quick blurb about having a package at the post office with a link that said *click here to see an image of your package.*

Zbirak could follow Robert Sherman home from work, but that always posed a risk of being caught in the act. Rose had probably already made contact, so Bob was likely aware of her situation. If he'd decided to help her—and a family man like him would—then he'd be on high alert if he understood even a fraction of the danger his late cousin's wife was in.

Sending an innocuous text was much less work and much less suspicious. Undoubtedly, curiosity would get the better of Bob Sherman, and he'd want to know more about the package. When he clicked on that link, it would take him to a page that never stopped buffering. Bob would wait for a moment or two, trying to see the package awaiting him, and in that time, Zbirak would get the information he needed to make his next move.

17

CASSIE OPENED THE ANNEX, LLC FOLDER ON HER LAP. THERE WERE maybe twenty sheets of paper inside. It looked like the company bought and sold property. They'd hold on to a piece of real estate for a month or two, then sell it again at a substantial increase in price.

"Something shady is going on there." Harris gestured to the folder.

Cassie nodded, flipping through the papers one at a time. "This address and phone number is listed on almost all the transactions."

"Let me see." Harris pulled out her phone and dialed the number. After a second, she put it on speaker.

"...trying to dial is temporarily unavailable. Please try again later."

"Wonder why," Cassie asked.

Harris shrugged. "Numbers like this get shut down all the time. Or changed. They gotta stay one step ahead of the cops."

"What about the address?" Cassie asked. "Wanna try that one?"

Harris grinned. "Thought you'd never ask."

Cassie navigated on her phone's GPS while Harris drove. They headed south, past the National Museum of Mexican Art and a few parks that would've made for a nice summer getaway. Cassie forgot the streets as soon as she read them out loud to Harris, but she did make a mental list of which monuments she'd love to revisit if they had time.

With lunchtime traffic, it took a half hour to get to where they needed to go. Harris pulled over about a block from the address. At that point, it would take less time to walk the rest of the way than continue to waste away in traffic. Despite the constant chill, Cassie found she was getting used to Chicago weather. But she still missed home.

"There's something about Reed that doesn't sit right with me," Cassie said.

Harris snorted. "Just one thing?"

"Well, no. A lot of things."

"How he could even find anything in that office is beyond me."

"Controlled chaos, I guess."

"There was nothing controlled about it."

"It was kind of warm in there," Cassie said, after a moment of silence.

"I didn't notice." Harris shrugged, but then cast a glance at Cassie. "You mean supernaturally warm?"

"I think so. It was hard to tell."

"Did you smell smoke?"

"I couldn't smell anything past that janitor's mop water." The pair of them turned the corner onto the next block. Cassie looked down at her phone, then pointed dead ahead. "It's halfway down this street."

"That janitor, too." Harris gave Cassie a nod of acknowledgment. "He was intense."

"I thought it was just me."

"Definitely not." A garbage truck pulled up to the side of the street, and a man jumped out. Harris paused until they were out of earshot. "It doesn't take a genius detective or a psychic consultant to see there's something shady going on."

"We're not going to get any information from either of them, though." Cassie looked back down at her phone and came to a halt. "Wait a second, we passed it."

Cassie turned back around, and Harris followed. This time,

Cassie paid closer attention to the numbers on the office buildings. She only stopped when she stood in front of a brand-new building. She looked over at Harris. "I think this is it."

"Or it *was*, anyway."

The building was nothing but framework and caution tape. Why they were trying to build it in the middle of winter was anyone's guess. Regardless, Cassie couldn't get a read off it. Most of the buildings around Chicago were older and had stories to tell. Even if those stories were nothing more than whispers, she could feel them around her. This one, however, was dead silent.

Harris looked around and spotted the garbage man. She gave him a friendly wave as she approached him, Cassie in tow. "Sorry to bother you." She flashed a smile and pointed to the building behind them. "But I was wondering if you know what happened to this building?"

The garbage man assessed the two of them before answering. He was a large man with tan skin and a scraggly beard. He seemed nice enough, though Cassie was pretty sure he could lift her up with one hand and toss her clear across the street. "It was condemned last year."

"Really?" Harris turned on all her innocent charm. "Do you know why?"

"Other than it being an eyesore?" He shrugged and went back to emptying the public garbage can. "No clue. Used to be a restaurant, then it got new owners. I think they turned it into an office building but can't really remember. Didn't last long. They knocked it down over the summer. Now they're turning it into something else."

"Any idea what?"

"Not a clue. Sorry." He sounded like he meant it.

"That's okay. Thanks anyway."

Harris and Cassie stood off to one side and looked up at the scaffolding. Cassie shook her head. "It feels like our luck is running out," she said. "And we didn't have much of that to begin with."

Harris's phone chimed. When she pulled it out of her pocket, her face erupted into a grin. "Maybe not." She held the phone out for

Cassie to see, but Cassie didn't recognize the number. "Local call," she said, then held the phone to her ear. "Hello?"

Cassie watched as Harris's face turned serious. When the detective responded in rapid-fire Spanish, Cassie knew who the other person was. Mrs. Carrera, the woman from the moving company, seemed to have had a change of heart.

Fewer than sixty seconds later, Harris hung up. She was already turning around and heading back the way they'd come. "Mrs. Carrera," Harris confirmed.

"What did she say?"

"The kid who stole the truck is her son. She said she knew it was him, and that's why she never reported it missing. She doesn't want him to get in trouble, but she does want me to kick his ass."

Cassie laughed. "She said that?"

"More or less. Said he needs a wake-up call." Harris was practically jogging back to the car. "But she made me promise not to arrest him. She gave me the address where he's been hanging out."

Cassie had trouble keeping up with the detective's pace. "Does she know why he stole it?"

"If she does, she didn't say. They've been having money trouble. She and her husband spent all their savings buying those trucks, and the business isn't doing as well as they'd hoped."

Realization dawned on Cassie. "He's trying to help them."

Harris nodded. "Whatever he's up to, I don't think he's doing it because he wants to."

Cassie finished her thought. "He's doing it because he thinks he has no other choice."

18

Chicago's South Side had a reputation for income disparity and crime, having gotten worse over the years. The divide between the more affluent areas and the streets and buildings that had been ignored was obvious. Having grown up in Montana, Harris had little experience with city life. Her family had been financially comfortable —not rich, but not poor.

When she was younger, she had struggled with her identity. Her mother, whose golden-brown skin was always dark, even in the winter, had been happy that her daughter could pass. *You'll have more opportunities this way, mija. It's a good thing.*

It had felt like a good thing. Until she went off to college and met all different kinds of people from around the world. Her roommate was from West Africa. Down the hall, a pair of twins from Argentina. The RA was from Mexico and went back every summer to stay with her family. Surrounded by a culture she should have recognized and didn't, it had made her feel twice as out of place.

Embracing the change, she did her homework. She got interested in who she was. When she went home, she asked her mother a thousand questions. She wanted to know more about where they came from and what their family had experienced in Puerto Rico. Her father was encouraging, and eventually, Harris began to feel like herself.

Of course, when she decided to be a cop, she had to set her identity aside again. But that was different. That was survival instinct. It was her choice to bury that part of her. Not from shame or ignorance. She saw how the old guys at work treated anyone different from them and understood she didn't need to fight another battle on a different front. Not when they were supposed to be on the same side.

But Chicago reminded her that the world wasn't fair and that she had gotten lucky. The people here didn't have a choice. The system kept them down, no matter how many times they tried to stand up and fight back. And those kinds of people got desperate. That was part of why she wanted to be a cop—not everyone who committed a crime was a bad person. She wanted to help them see there was another way.

Cassie pointed ahead. "See that tan building up there?" She looked back down at her phone and up again. "I think that's it."

Harris pulled over. "I wish I knew what we were getting into here." She drummed her fingers on the steering wheel. "His mom didn't say much. Just that he hung out here sometimes. And that she didn't like these boys very much."

Cassie gulped. "He's not going to help us if he's trying to impress his friends."

"My thoughts exactly." Harris checked her side view mirror, then stepped into the street, slamming the door shut behind her. The air was crisp, biting at her nose and cheeks and reminding her she'd made the right call bringing her heavier jacket. The weight of the coat continued to brush against her injured arm, and she had to resist the urge to rub the pain away. "Just stay close and let me do the talking. I might have to improv."

Cassie's voice was dripping with sarcasm when she responded. "How exciting."

The building looked like an apartment complex, four stories tall and in desperate need of renovation. Half the windows on the first floor were boarded up, and even a few on the second had planks of wood across them. If she didn't know any better, she would've thought it was abandoned.

Someone emerged from the front of the building, looking agitated. When he stepped onto the sidewalk, he threw both middle fingers up at someone inside. Harris squinted, trying to make out his face. When he turned and leaned against the building, pulling a joint out of his pocket, she caught a good glimpse of him.

"Armando?" she asked. He looked up at the sound of his name, the joint halfway to his lips. "Armando Carrera?"

That was all the prompting he needed. Armando flicked the joint into the street and took off. Harris's reaction was immediate. She'd been trained to go from zero to full speed at the drop of a hat. "Stay with the car!" she called over her shoulder. Hearing Cassie's protests, she ignored them.

The kid was fast, she'd give him that. And he knew these streets better than she did. But he was used to making a quick getaway and hiding until his pursuers gave up the chase. All she had to do was keep him in her sights and run him down. She didn't do cardio six days a week for nothing.

Armando also made the mistake of looking over his shoulder every ten or fifteen seconds. It slowed him down considerably, and at the junction of one street and the next, he almost ran head first into an elderly man in a suit. The kid dodged out of the way at the last second, eliciting a sharp curse from the man. Harris didn't bother apologizing on his behalf. Leaning into her sprint, she knew that every mistake he made closed the distance between them.

Harris wondered if he recognized her from the jewelry shop, or if he was running because that was the smartest thing to do when someone called out his full name. She'd sounded too much like a cop, and it had intimidated him.

Coming up on another street corner, Harris could feel her body adjusting to the pace. Her lungs were just starting to burn, but the real problem was the cold air hitting her eyes and making them water. She blinked away the tears, afraid that if she took her eyes off

Armando for a split second, he'd disappear, and she'd never find him again.

It was that panicked thought that drove Harris forward, pushing her legs past her limit and hoping they'd hold out. She was a strong runner, built for distance more than speed, but even she had her breaking point. And Armando was proving to have as much stamina as she did. Taking a sudden left, he ran through traffic. Cars honked and squealed their tires as Harris followed. But where he had found an opening to dash between vehicles, she had to dodge and swerve, pausing in the middle of the street while an old man shook his fist at her. When Armando made it to the sidewalk on the other side, he ran about a hundred feet back up the street and slipped into an alleyway. Harris yelled in frustration, then followed in his wake, ignoring the people yelling at her from both inside their cars and on foot.

There was nothing like a jolt of anger for that extra boost of speed. Sometimes it was even better than adrenaline, and Harris relied on it to get the upper hand. As her feet hit the pavement in time behind him, Armando made the mistake of looking over his shoulder one more time to see how far away she was. Tripping on a pothole, he stumbled. He recovered, but it had closed the gap between them considerably.

And as they reached the end of the alley, Harris reached out her arm to grab the back of his sweatshirt just as a gold Toyota Corolla hopped the curb and cut them off. Armando slammed into the car and tumbled over the hood, then hit the sidewalk on the other side. Harris jumped just in time to slide across the front of the car, dropping down next to him and grabbing a fistful of his shirt before he could hop up and run away again.

When the driver's side door opened, Cassie stepped out, grinning from ear to ear. Harris couldn't help the frustration that mounted inside her chest. "Didn't I tell you to stay with the car?"

Cassie still wore a shit-eating grin on her face. "Technically," she said, gesturing to the car, "I did."

19

Cassie returned to the steering wheel after Harris shoved Armando into the backseat and slid in beside him. She had no idea where they were going and didn't bother asking. It was better if it looked like she knew what she was doing. Besides, she needed to get the car off the sidewalk before the cops showed up.

Looking at him in the rearview mirror, Cassie could see how much Armando looked like the older woman they'd seen the night before. Their eyes were the same shape, as were their noses and lips. There was no doubt this was Mrs. Carrera's son, but the real question was whether he took after her in other ways. Would he shut down like his mother did when they asked questions?

As soon as Armando got to the other side of the seat, he reached for the doorhandle. But Cassie was faster. Locking the doors, she turned on the child lock for good measure. When he glared at her, she gave a sheepish smile in return.

"This will go much smoother if you cooperate," Harris said.

"I'm not telling you shit," Armando said, sounding much tougher than he had the other day in the jewelry store. "Arrest me. I don't care. You've got nothing on me."

"Oh, we're not going to arrest you." Harris's grin stretched her whole face. "We're taking you back to your mom's place." She turned to Cassie. "Remember how to get there?"

"Oh yeah." Cassie didn't remember how to get there, but she pulled her phone out of her pocket and figured out an approximation of where to go. Then she pulled into the street and merged with the flow of traffic. Staring at Armando through the rearview mirror again, she said, "Twenty minutes, give or take."

Armando's eyes went wide. Looking over at Harris, his gruff exterior fell away. "Come on, lady. What'd I do to you? Please don't take me back there. She's gonna whoop my ass."

"We'll drop you off wherever you need to go," Harris said, "as long as you answer my questions."

Armando groaned. "I don't know anything."

"I'm sure you know something." Harris's grin never faded. She was enjoying messing with him like this. "Do you recognize me?" She pointed at Cassie. "Either one of us?"

"Yeah, you were at the jewelry store."

"So were you. Why?"

Armando shrugged and stayed cautious. "Just doing my job."

"And what job is that?"

"My family owns a moving company."

"See, I might have believed you if I hadn't already talked to your mom. She said you stole the moving truck."

"I didn't steal it."

Harris laughed. "I've got nowhere to be for the rest of the night, Armando. And I'm very patient."

"I didn't steal it," Armando repeated. "Just borrowed it."

"Without permission."

"Yeah."

"That's stealing."

"I was going to return it. I just needed it for a job."

"Now we're back to my original question." Harris's voice was getting less and less congenial. "What job was that?"

Cassie stopped at a red light and watched as Armando weighed his options. It didn't look good either way, and he must've come to that conclusion too. Sweat beaded along his hairline and across his top lip, even though the car's heat was on its lowest setting.

Armando's answer was reluctant. "Picking up furniture and other stuff."

"What other stuff?"

"Whatever we could find. We were supposed to clean it out." He rushed on, nervous. "Not, like, jewelry. That was all gone when we got there. Furniture and garbage. Shitty stuff that wasn't worth anything."

"Why were you picking it up if it wasn't worth anything?"

"I don't know." When Harris leveled him with a look, he held up his hands. "Honest, I don't know. No one told me anything."

"Who's they? The man you were with?"

Cassie glanced at Armando through the mirror again. He was looking at his hands in his lap.

"Armando," Harris warned. "You need to tell me."

"Look, I know he doesn't look like much, but he's a scary dude."

"I'll make sure he doesn't do anything to you."

Armando scoffed. "No offense, lady, but I'd rather be on your bad side than his."

"Fair enough. I'm not looking to get you in trouble here. Don't say who your partner is, but I'm gonna need to know somebody's name."

"I don't have any other names." After another hard look from Harris, he buckled down. "Really. That guy from the shop is just some dude my friend knows. When I told my buddy I needed cash, he hooked me up. Old man said I'd get forty percent if I could get the truck for a day."

"And you didn't ask what he needed you to do?"

"Figured the less I knew, the better."

"That's very inconvenient for us, Armando."

He sighed. "Look, I've only ever seen him talk to one other person. Another scary looking guy covered in tattoos." He rushed on before Harris could ask. "I don't know his name."

"Can you describe any of the tattoos?"

"The one on his forearm looked like a mermaid. She was naked."

Cassie rolled her eyes. Of course, a tattoo like that would stick out to a teenage boy.

"Anything else?" Harris asked.

"No." Armando sounded impatient now. "Can you please drop me off? If they figure out I talked, they'll kill me."

"You don't know anything," Harris reassured him. "I'm sure they'd be a lot worse to us than to you."

The idea didn't comfort Cassie, but she kept her mouth shut as she turned the next corner.

"Still—"

"One last question," Harris said. "Where's the truck?"

Cassie's gaze flicked back to the mirror, and she saw Armando warring with himself.

"I can't—"

"You need to tell us." Harris's voice was low now. Sincere. "It's important. One of our friends, he—" She stuttered to a stop, then took a deep breath before she continued. "He was murdered, and we think it has something to do with that jewelry store. No reason to get you in trouble if you weren't responsible. We just want to know why someone would want him dead. He was a good person, Armando, and he didn't deserve to die."

Something in Harris's voice must've hit a nerve with Armando because a few seconds later, he was rattling off an address, and Harris punched it into her phone. It was perfect timing, too, because they had pulled into the Carreras' driveway.

Armando shrunk down in his seat. Mrs. Carrera was already standing in the doorway, with twin looks of relief and fury warring on her face. "She's going to kill me."

Cassie turned off the child lock, and Harris leaned across Armando to push open his door. "I'd start begging for forgiveness, then."

"You said you would take me wherever I wanted to go!"

"No." Harris wore her best impression of a pre-school teacher handing out a tough lesson. "I said we'd take you wherever you *needed* to go."

20

As suspected, Bob Sherman's curiosity got the better of him. After Zbirak sent the text message with the image link, it only took the man another half an hour before he opened it. He proceeded to reload it three more times when the image of his mysterious package wouldn't populate. It was more than enough for Zbirak to infiltrate the man's phone and learn anything and everything about him and his movements around the city.

First, Zbirak connected the phone's GPS location to his computer. Now, he could see exactly where Bob was and predict where he would go next. Then Zbirak logged into the man's calendar. So many people thought technology was their saving grace.

It was only when Zbirak scrolled through Bob Sherman's contacts that his plan started to form. It was too easy, given all the information Bob thought was safe for the keeping. But easy was good. Easy was smart. There had been too many mistakes so far, and it was time for Zbirak to correct them all.

If Bob Sherman knew where Rose was, Zbirak was about to find out.

The first order of the day was to ditch his current car for a clean one. Despite Chicago's size and the unlikeliness of getting caught,

Zbirak thought it'd be better not to take any chances. He used one of his many forms of identification, as well as a clean credit card, to rent a car for the week—a sleek black Jeep Cherokee that smelled like pine trees. As far as rentals went, he'd had far worse.

The next stop was downtown, around where Bob Sherman worked. It was a large building with the words *Madison Investment Co.* on the front in gold letters. It was a bit flashy for Zbirak's taste, but Bob had done well at the company over the years, and he seemed happy. At least, as happy as one could be, working for a heartless corporate monster.

In fact, today was a big day for Bob, and Zbirak had to admit it couldn't have worked out any better. He liked the phrase *regression to the mean*. It made him feel better about the future when everything else had gone to shit. Rose's escape had been unfortunate, but the universe had to balance itself out sooner or later. And it looked like today would be his lucky day.

Bob had an important meeting at three o'clock in which he would get promoted. It had not taken long for Zbirak to find his way into the company's email system to confirm that, yes, Bob would receive good news today. Text messages between him and his wife confirmed he was hopeful, albeit nervous, and that no, he would not forget his son had a play at six o'clock that evening.

Little Georgie would be portraying the donkey in the annual Christmas Nativity play. It was a role for the ages, he'd said. Their son's big break. Bob would be there, camera in hand, no matter what.

Zbirak hoped that was true, for Georgie's sake, more than Bob's, but he had a feeling the rest of the evening would be spent in far less glamorous conditions. Then again, that was up to Bob.

Street parking was a nightmare, but Zbirak had an ace up his sleeve. He'd used his access to Bob's emails to print himself a pass for the parking garage underneath the building. After that, it was just a game of patience as he found which spot Bob had taken that day. The area had filled up fast, but Zbirak managed to find one across from the man's little navy-blue Hyundai Sonata.

An hour later, Bob sent off texts to his wife, his brother-in-law, and half a dozen friends. They all responded within a matter of minutes, congratulating him on his hard work. His wife was particularly graphic in how they would celebrate later that evening, and Zbirak gave them a few moments of privacy before he looked for any relevant information among the filth.

Then he went back to the emails. Publicly, many of Bob's coworkers sent him congratulatory messages. Privately, several of them fumed at having been passed over for the promotion. Zbirak wondered if they would feel guilty for their jealousy and greed if Bob never returned to work. Once the police gained access to the emails, would any of them be suspects?

After begging off from several invites to go grab a drink, Bob left Madison Investment fifteen minutes early. Zbirak was practically vibrating in his seat with anticipation. Everything had lined up perfectly. After the mess of the last job, he knew this would go over smoothly as long as he stuck to the plan. Zbirak had to be careful of any vehicles descending from the floors above, but it really was an ideal situation. He needed Bob alone, and the universe had given him just that.

Bob emerged from the elevator with his head bent over his phone. He unlocked his car with several dozen feet yet to go. Women were so much more vigilant, and Zbirak shook his head in disappointment. It's not like Bob was a large man. He would be no challenge at all.

Zbirak exited his vehicle and stalked toward his prey. Just as they were about to pass, he infused his voice with as much cheerfulness as he could muster. It was not difficult, given his projected evening. "Hey, Bob. How're you doing?"

Bob looked up, and Zbirak could see him trying to grasp for his name. "Hey, man." He paused again. "Good, good. How are you?"

"Could be better." Zbirak forced a frown as he stopped and faced the other man. Etiquette told Bob he also had to stop and listen to what he had to say. "Picking up my last paycheck. Can't believe I got fired."

"Oh no." Bob looked more interested in the drama than anything. "What happened?"

"They had to make room for some higher up's promotion. Can you believe that? Said there was nothing wrong with my work, they just couldn't afford the guy's demands without letting some people go." Zbirak really had to fight against a grin now. "My kid's sick. I don't know where I'm gonna be able to find a new job so quickly."

"Oh." Bob's face fell. "Well, I'm sure there's something, man. It's Christmastime. Everyone's hiring."

"Yeah, but they don't pay as much, you know?"

"Yeah."

Zbirak let the silence hang in the air until it felt awkward. He could see Bob itching to go. "Hey, you heading to Lincoln Elementary? Bet your kid's gonna be real cute."

Bob's eyebrows pinched together. "I'm sorry. I'm having a hard time thinking of your name. What was it again?"

Zbirak really did smile this time. "Joe." He hated that name, but it was far more disarming. "Don't you remember me?"

"Joe, right." Bob nodded like he remembered. "Up in accounting, right?"

"That's right. Joe from accounting."

Maybe it was something in Zbirak's voice or the fact that Bob was smarter than he looked, but the other man's face fell. "There's no Joe in accounting, man."

"Ah." Zbirak let the façade fall away, and he noticed the exact second Bob knew he was in trouble. "You caught on much faster than I thought you would."

Bob backed up toward his car. "What do you want?"

"I want to know where Rose is."

"Who?" Bob had the wherewithal to feign innocence. "I don't know a Rose."

"Don't lie to me, Robert." Zbirak allowed a little bit of a growl to enter his voice. It had the desired effect. "Or little Georgie will grow up without his daddy."

Bob froze. "What have you done to him?"

"Nothing." Zbirak placed a hand over his heart, offended. "I don't hurt kids unless I have to. You, on the other hand, are fair game. And so is your wife."

Bob didn't bother asking any more questions. He turned and sprinted toward his car. But Zbirak was faster. Within two strides, he caught the other man around the neck and held him against his chest. A smile spread across his face. His plan had gone perfectly, just like he'd predicted.

"Let's have a little chat," Zbirak whispered. "Shall we?"

21

Cassie and Harris stuck around long enough to switch seats in the car. Neither was keen to find out what would happen to Armando now that they had returned him home. Mrs. Carrera's relief lasted only a few seconds before she ordered him inside and laid into him. Cassie didn't need to understand Spanish to know he was in mountains of trouble.

Harris took the most direct route to the warehouse. They arrived in under thirty minutes, despite the evening traffic.

The warehouse looked more like an old industrial factory. It was made of brick and had a tall smokestack off to one side. In the waning light, Cassie could see dozens of broken windows. It looked abandoned.

They parked the car a block away and got out to walk. Cassie almost missed the heat from the jewelry store as outdoor temperatures fell and the warm sun disappeared. At least then she would've been able to feel her fingers. "What do you expect we'll find in here?"

"The truck, hopefully." Harris kept her head on a swivel, but the area looked dead. "And that filing cabinet."

"The empty filing cabinet?"

"The clearly important filing cabinet that must have some significance."

"What if the folders were important, but they're gone now? Then this is just another dead end."

Harris put a reassuring hand on Cassie's shoulder. "Investigating *is* a lot of dead ends. You have to play process of elimination before you find the right lead."

Cassie rubbed her hands together and blew into them. "Wish we'd find the right one sooner rather than later."

Harris stayed silent as they approached the building from the side. No one milled about, and no noises came from inside. With any luck, they wouldn't run into anyone. But Harris wouldn't have anyone to interrogate, either. Cassie was trying not to give up hope, but their days were running out. She missed her house and her cat and her dog and everything about Savannah. Including David.

"Could we be so lucky?" Harris approached a door on the side of the building and tugged on the handle. "Guess not. You stay here. I'm going to have a quick look around."

Cassie scoffed. "Why can't I come with you?"

"Because this is the main thoroughfare," Harris said, pointing to the road behind them. "I want to know if anyone shows up. I'll be back in a minute. You'll be fine."

Cassie rolled her eyes but didn't argue. Before she knew it, Harris had slipped around the corner. But it was too cold to just stand out here, jumping up and down, trying to get her blood flowing to all her extremities. She looked for another option. And that's when she spotted it.

A window to the left of the door, about six feet up. It was an odd place for it, and Cassie wondered if it had been used for ventilation more than anything else. The glass was broken and jagged. Harris had likely dismissed it because it would've been difficult to get into without hurting themselves. But Cassie spotted a pipe on the ground long enough to reach it. She used the pipe to knock out the rest of the glass and sweep it onto the ground. When she was satisfied, she tossed the pipe to the side and leapt up to grab the ledge of the window.

The glass pressed into the palms of her hand, but it didn't break the skin. Her upper body strength was minimal, but the last few months of exercise and adventure had proven useful. She pulled herself up, feet scrambling against the side of the building, until she could peek inside. It took a few seconds for her eyes to adjust to the darkness, but she didn't see anyone.

By then, her arms were shaking from exhaustion, and she was forced to let go and drop back to the ground. She carefully wiped the glass from her palms and tried again, this time pulling herself up faster than before. She managed to hook one elbow along the inside wall, and that was enough to bring most of her torso through the opening. After that, it was only a matter of swinging her legs through and dropping to the floor inside.

Cassie froze as her landing echoed around the warehouse. The darkness consumed her. For a second, her mind conjured all sorts of people stepping from the shadows, ready to attack her.

As her eyesight adjusted, she realized she was alone.

The warehouse was huge, and looked much larger without all its former equipment inside. The dust tickled her nose, but she fought the urge to sneeze. If someone *was* here, there was no doubt they could hear her.

Debris littered the floor. Old planks of wood, waterlogged and half rotten. Nuts and bolts, nails and screws. Beer bottles and Coke cans. There were even little piles of dirt here and there, like someone had tried to clean the place up and realized it was a losing battle.

Cassie stepped closer to the nearest pile of dirt. On top was a pamphlet, just like the ones they'd seen in the jewelry store. She wondered if Harris would come across the truck parked out back.

There was a sudden hissing noise, and Cassie crouched lower to the ground. It was coming from outside, and it sounded like—

"Cassie?"

It was just Harris, looking for her. Cassie stood and stepped to the door, sliding back the deadbolt. But when she pulled the door open, she found herself looking down the barrel of a gun.

Harris swore and lowered it. "Jesus, Cassie. What the hell?"

"I found a way inside."

"I could've shot you."

"I'm glad you didn't."

Harris shook her head and entered, closing the door behind them. She lowered her voice. "How?"

Cassie pointed up at the window. "Figured I'd give it a try."

"Next time, wait for me?"

"Next time, don't leave me behind."

Harris shot her a look, but turned to the rest of the room. "Did you find anything?"

Cassie held up the pamphlet. "From the jewelry store."

"I saw the truck out back. Figured we were in the right place. Glad Armando didn't try to screw us with a wrong address. There were a few more cars, too. There might be people upstairs. Have you heard anything?"

Cassie was only half paying attention. She raised a hand and pointed to the far corner of the warehouse. "Those look like our filing cabinets."

They were lined up against the back wall. It was the most organized section of the entire building. Cassie wondered who put them here, and why they cared so much about these filing cabinets and not the rest of the space.

She pulled out her phone and snapped a picture. A chill traveled down her spine while a featherlight touch of heat brushed past her cheek. She could see a shadow hovering next to the cabinet at the end. It looked thicker than the surrounding darkness. Three-dimensional.

She held the phone out for Harris.

"That's terrifying," Harris said.

"It's not here to hurt us."

"Hey, you're the expert. I'm just the muscle."

Cassie walked up to the cabinet and touched the handle of the top drawer and immediately pulled back. "It's ice cold."

"Well, it's not like the building has great insulation." Harris swept an arm toward all the broken windows.

How could Cassie explain it felt colder than normal? That the moment she touched it, ice had enveloped her hand and pulled her closer, as if it never wanted her to let go.

Cassie moved on to the next drawer, only slightly warmer. The next one down felt normal. Beneath that, the metal was nearly warm to the touch. Only when she got to the fifth drawer did she realize this was the one they'd been searching for. It was scorching.

Using the sleeve of her jacket, she pulled it open. Harris leaned forward to look inside. "Empty."

"It has to be this one." Cassie stuck her hand inside, hoping she could feel what she couldn't see. "There's no other explanation."

"Do ghosts ever play practical jokes on you?"

Cassie glared up at her. "No."

Harris raised her hands in surrender. "Just wondering."

A clang and a crash made them jump. Voices drifted forward from the opposite end of the warehouse, but they couldn't make out any words. One of the few pieces of machinery that hadn't been moved was the only thing between them and the newcomers.

Harris yanked open the top drawer, then methodically moved through them one at a time. But they were all empty. She swore again. "Are you sure—?"

"Yes, I'm sure," Cassie hissed. "It's this one. I know it is."

Harris reached past her and pulled hard enough on the handle that the whole cabinet wobbled. There was a loud screech as the metal ground against the concrete below. The voices stopped. Harris let go of the drawer.

"We have to leave. Now," Harris said.

Cassie shook her head. "Not yet. I know this is it."

With a pounding heart, Cassie got down on her hands and knees and peered into the drawer one last time. Harris must've shaken something loose because at the very back of the cabinet, between its outer wall and the back of the drawer, was a crumpled file. It had slipped down behind a drawer. This was it. This was what the ghost had been trying to tell her about.

"Cassie, come on."

"I see something."

She stuck her arm inside the drawer and grabbed the file. It was crushed and twisted and starting to rip. But she didn't have time to be gentle. She pulled, and after a second's hesitation, the file folded and sprang free. Cassie almost cheered in victory.

Harris grabbed her wrist and pulled her along the back wall. They hid behind a stack of empty pallets. Cassie could hardly control her breathing as a group of men approached the filing cabinets. She had closed all the drawers but the bottom one.

There was a beat of silence before one guy spoke.

"Looks like someone's poking their nose where it don't belong."

22

Cassie held her breath as she listened to the group of men standing just a few feet away from their hiding spot. It sounded like there were at least four or five.

Someone popped open a can, and Cassie could hear him chugging from where she was crouched behind the pallets. He let out a massive belch before talking. "Those pieces of junk were empty, anyway. What's it matter?"

"It matters because I said it matters," the first guy said. None of the others argued.

Harris bent down and picked up a chunk of broken metal off the ground. The detective scuttled forward until Cassie was sure someone would see her, then reared her arm back and lobbed the piece of metal over the guys' heads. When it landed, it must've hit something metallic because the collision echoed around the building with a tinny ring.

"Go, go!" the first guy shouted, and Cassie heard the group race toward the other end of the building. She didn't have time to think about what to do next before Harris grabbed her wrist and hauled her toward the door.

But one of the guys must've stayed back to keep an eye on the filing cabinets because as soon as they emerged from behind the pallets, Cassie heard one of them give a surprised, "Hey!"

"Don't look back," Harris hissed, tightening her grip around Cassie's wrist.

Cassie had no desire to disobey orders. She kept an eye on her feet and made sure she didn't trip over anything while the detective dragged her along. By the time they made it to the door, the others had realized they'd fallen for the trap and started shouting after them.

But it was too late. Harris burst through the door with Cassie on her heels. As soon as the detective dropped her arm, Cassie scooped up the metal pipe she'd used to break the window and shoved it through the handle to lock the door from the outside. There were plenty of other exits, but at least it would slow the men down.

By the time they reached the car, Cassie was wheezing and her fingers were so frozen, she could barely operate the door handle. When she did finally crawl inside, Harris didn't bother turning on the heat. She put the car in drive and hit the gas.

Cassie slammed back into her seat, scrambling for her seatbelt. "Where are we going?"

"Away from here." Harris checked her rearview and visibly relaxed. "I don't want them to know who's been poking around."

"What if they saw the car already?"

"We'll deal with that when it comes back to bite us in the ass." She threw a significant look at the folder on Cassie's lap. "Go on, let's see what's so important."

Before Cassie could so much as reach for the folder, her phone started buzzing. "It's Jason," she said. Cassie got her breath back under control before she answered. "Hello?"

"Hey, what's going on?" Jason asked.

"Not much." She looked back at the warehouse diminishing in the distance. "You know, just a typical day."

"Typical, huh? Are you safe?"

"Always." Cassie hated lying to Jason, but there was no point in getting him worked up. "You got something for me?"

"Actually, yeah. Harris with you?"

"Yeah. Hang on." Cassie put Jason on speaker, then cranked up the heat until it was blasting her in the face. "Go ahead."

"Detective."

"Jason."

Cassie didn't let their awkwardness hang in the air any longer than necessary. "Did you find something out about Don Reed?"

"Nothing you couldn't already guess. Plenty of arrests. No convictions. He's had his hands in a lot of dealings over the years, and most of them have been less than reputable."

"How has he stayed out of trouble, then?" Cassie asked.

"Not sure. He seems like a sneaky bastard, for one. He knows how to make the law work for him. And when he can't, he finds someone to be his patsy." Jason paused for more questions, but when neither Harris nor Cassie spoke up, he continued. "That's not why I'm calling, though."

"You have other news?" Harris asked.

"Cassie told you about Rose Sherman's house?"

"She did. Did you find out who did it?"

"No. They didn't leave anything behind, and the police have no leads, as far as I'm aware."

"As far as you're aware?" Harris shot Jason a questioning look through the phone. "You have an insider?"

"Oh, um." Jason cleared his throat. "Not exactly. But I have friends who know people."

"Right. Best we leave it at that."

"Yeah. Anyway." He cleared his throat again. "Turns out Rose booked a flight to Chicago, of all places."

Harris and Cassie looked at each other with raised eyebrows. Cassie leaned closer to the phone. "You're sure? Why would she be heading here?"

"I did some digging, and it turns out her husband has a cousin living in Chicago. His name is Robert Sherman. He's an investment broker. Has a wife and a kid in elementary school."

"Is he connected with Aguilar?" Harris asked.

"I don't think so. At least, not that I could find. But the investment banking—"

"Is definitely worth some digging."

"I'll keep looking." There was a hint of pride in Jason's voice, like he wanted nothing more than to help them on their quest to get answers about all of this. "If I find anything, I'll let you know."

"And the cousin's address?" Harris asked.

"Sending it now."

Cassie hung up and waited for the address to come through. She put it into her phone's GPS, then looked back up at Harris. "It's back north. In Evanston. It's gonna take at least an hour to get there."

"Then we shouldn't waste any time." Harris checked her mirrors, making sure the coast was clear. She cranked the wheel to the left, cutting across the road and straightening up the car until they were facing the opposite direction. "If she landed this morning, we might be ahead of whoever's chasing her."

Cassie looked down at the folder in her lap. It felt like it was burning a hole through her legs, though that was more metaphorical than literal this time. She wondered if the shadow had followed them. Was it sitting in the backseat, waiting to see where they would go next? She resisted the urge to turn around and look.

Cassie looked back down at the file in her lap. "So much trouble to get this."

"Would be a shame to not see what the big deal is."

Cassie bit her lip, caught between knowing they needed to take the next step and still feeling as though they were playing a dangerous game. Every cell in her body was screaming that it was a bad idea. It was easier to ignore it. "Here goes." She flipped the folder open and scanned the first page. "Looks like insurance claims?"

Harris tried to keep her eyes on the road and the folder at the same time. "What kind of insurance claims?" She swerved, and two different cars honked their horns.

"You focus on getting us to Robert Sherman's house alive," Cassie said. She jabbed a finger at the folder. "I'll try to figure out what's going on here."

They made it to Evanston in record time. Cassie's head was swimming with names and numbers and timelines, but she wasn't sure she knew any more than she did an hour ago.

All thoughts of the folder left her mind when they pulled into Robert Sherman's driveway.

"No car in the driveway," Harris said.

Cassie leaned forward to get a better look at the house. It was a beautiful ranch with blue siding and manicured gardens covered in snow. The roof had sharp peaks, smart for the winter. It wasn't a flashy house by any means, but out here it was worth a pretty penny.

Harris whistled as she got out of the car. "Couldn't afford that on my salary."

"Think Robert can?"

"Probably, but let's see what the inside looks like before we judge."

Harris led the way along the lantern-lit sidewalk, then up the stairs, until she was knocking on the front door. Cassie hadn't thought to ask her what the plan was. How would they get any information out of this guy? What if he truly didn't know anything?

But before she could ask, the door was opening.

The woman standing before them looked like she was having a rough day. Her blonde bob, which had probably been sharp and smooth that morning, was a wild mess, like she'd been running her hands through it. With red-rimmed eyes and a tissue in one hand, it wasn't hard to guess that she'd been crying. She looked at the two of them, like she couldn't possibly imagine why they'd be there.

Harris found her voice first. "Mrs. Sherman?"

"Yes?"

"My name is Adelaide Harris. This is my associate, Cassie Quinn. We're looking for your husband."

"Oh no." The woman's voice was quiet and shaky. "Is he in trouble? Is something wrong? Do you have any idea where he could be?"

"I was going to ask you the same thing," Harris said.

"He was supposed to go to our son's play after work. I was texting him, and then he just stopped answering." A sob escaped her throat.

"He's always on time. Always. And he never forgets. He would never forget—"

"Do you know if he's been in recent contact with Randall or Rose?"

The woman froze. "Who are you?"

"We're here to help."

It was all Harris said before she shouldered her way inside.

23

THE WOMAN GASPED AND SPUTTERED AS HARRIS AND CASSIE WALKED straight into the house, uninvited.

"What are you doing?" Mrs. Sherman pointed toward the door. "Get out."

"Does your husband have a home office?" Harris didn't want to wait for an answer. "I'll find it."

The woman gaped after her. Then, turning to Cassie, fear and anger and confusion in her eyes, asked. "What is she doing?"

"I'm so sorry about that." Cassie had her hands up in surrender. Her voice was soft and gentle. "Adelaide is a detective. We want to help you find your husband."

"A detective?" The woman paused, looking back over her shoulder as if she could verify it just by sight. "But I didn't call anyone."

"We're from Savannah."

"Georgia?"

Cassie nodded and saw the woman's confusion deepen. "We're here on another case. It led us to your husband."

"What? Why? Is he in trouble? Bob wouldn't—"

"No, no, he's not in trouble." Cassie didn't know if that was true but wasn't about to push her luck. "What's your name, by the way?" She held out her hand. "I'm Cassie."

"Melissa," the woman said. They shook hands. "I don't know if this is a good idea. Maybe I should call the police."

"You can," Cassie said, infusing her voice with reassurance despite that being the very last thing she wanted to happen. "Unfortunately, they won't be able to verify that we're here, since Adelaide isn't from their department."

"If she's the detective," Melissa said, slowly, "who are you?"

"Oh, um." Cassie took in the woman's living room for the first time, trying to find an item that would tell her more about the Shermans. It was clean and neat, with a cross on the wall above a picture of an older woman. Candles everywhere. Pictures in frames on every surface. "I'm a consultant."

"What does that mean? Are you a cop?"

"No. I do work with the Savannah PD on cases." Most definitely not a lie. "I've helped solve dozens of murders."

"Murder?" Tears began to streak down Melissa's face. "Do you think—"

"No, no. That's not why we're here. Well, it is. But not for your husband."

But the tears didn't stop. "What if he's dead? What if someone killed him? He never misses Georgie's events. Never."

"Where is your son right now?"

"Upstairs." The woman's tears slowed a little. "I had to work late today. We were supposed to meet at the school. But when I got there, they said Bob never showed up. I brought Georgie home right away. I didn't know what else to do. Thank goodness he has no idea what's going on."

"Good, good." Cassie gestured to the couch. "Can we sit? Would that be okay?"

Melissa nodded, but as soon as she sat down, stood up again and started pacing. "He could be dead. What if he is? Oh, God."

"Melissa, he's not dead." Cassie kept the annoyance out of her voice, but she needed to be firm, or they'd get nowhere. She hoped Harris was having better luck. "Are you sure he just didn't forget?"

"I'm sure. I was texting him. He got a promotion, so we were celebrating." She held out her phone so Cassie could see the conversation. It went back and forth for a while, and if Melissa was embarrassed by some of the more explicit texts, she didn't show it. "Then he just stops answering." There was a wall of blue text, one after the other, that got more panicked as time went on. "I called him, too, but he never answered. He *always* answers."

"If he got a promotion, maybe he went out drinking with his buddies?"

She shook her head so vigorously, Cassie could see the tears flying off her face. "Bob doesn't really like those guys. They're a bunch of backstabbers. He would've preferred to spend his time at home. With his family."

"We're going to find him." Cassie had a gut feeling those words were true, but she didn't know whether they'd find him dead or alive. "But I need to ask about his cousin, Randall. And Randall's wife."

Melissa stopped pacing. "Randall is not a good person. We stopped associating with them a long time ago."

"Randall is dead."

A myriad of emotions flashed across the other woman's face. Shock. Sadness. Regret. Resolve. "I told Bob his cousin would end up in prison or in a ditch someday." That resolve flickered for a moment. "But I'm sorry to hear it was the latter."

"What about Rose? Do you know anything about her?"

Melissa was already shaking her head. "I don't want to talk about this. I'm calling the police. You shouldn't be here."

"Wait!" Cassie stood. Harris hadn't emerged from the back of the house yet. She must've found a room to search but hadn't found what she was looking for—whatever that was. "Please, we need your help."

"You need to leave."

Cassie's eyes landed on the portrait of the older woman on the wall. She looked like Melissa, with the same gentle eyes and thin lips that turned down a little at the corners. "You were close with your mother, weren't you?"

Melissa froze. "What?"

"Your mother. She died recently." Cassie pointed to the portrait. There was no point in trying to deny she saw it. "I'm sure that was difficult."

"What's your point?"

What *was* her point? She was grasping at straws here. "I lost someone recently, too. A friend. My best friend." Tears, unbidden, gathered in her eyes. "That's why I'm here. Trying to figure out what happened to him."

"I'm sorry for your loss." It sounded sincere. "But I don't understand what that has to do—"

"I'm a psychic." Cassie hadn't meant to say it. Not like that, anyway. "I know it sounds crazy, but it's true. And it's important." The other woman stayed silent, so Cassie rushed on. "I am a consultant with the Savannah PD. A psychic consultant. Like I said, I've helped solve dozens of murders. But this one, David's murder, is different. He hasn't come to me like others have. And I don't know what to do. I don't know how to solve this."

"You're insane," Melissa whispered, but she said it like she was afraid it wasn't true.

"I don't think Bob is dead because I can't see him. Or feel him. Wherever he is, he's still alive."

Melissa's next words came out in a hiss. "How dare you—"

"Your mother." Cassie turned back to the portrait. "She died of breast cancer, didn't she?"

Melissa took a step back. "How did you know?"

Cassie had seen a pink ribbon pinned to the woman's coat next to the door. But she wasn't about to tell Melissa that. "You two went on a trip near the end, didn't you?" The portrait sitting next to the couch. Cassie had recognized the iconic façade of the Duomo. "Florence? She'd always wanted to go there, hadn't she?"

A strangled sob had escaped Melissa's mouth. Shuffling over to the couch, she sat down, like her legs could barely hold her weight anymore. "Is she here?"

Cassie closed her eyes. She didn't want to lie or cause this woman more pain, but she needed answers and she needed to find Bob before something happened. "Yes. She says it was the best time of her life."

"I miss her so much." Melissa was sobbing now, her face in her hands. "Every day."

"She misses you, too. But she's happy." Cassie hated herself a little. But it wasn't a lie. This is what people wanted to hear. Sometimes it didn't matter if it was true or not. "Your mother is at peace. She doesn't want you to waste your life missing her. She wants you to keep going. For your husband. For little Georgie."

Melissa looked up at Cassie. Tears streamed down her face, and she licked them away from her lips. Hope burned brightly in her eyes. "It's hard."

Cassie knelt in front of Melissa and put her hand on the woman's knee. "I know. She knows. But it's time. You've grieved long enough."

Melissa swallowed back a sob long enough to speak. "Thank you."

"You're welcome." Cassie hoped her words comforted the woman. "I can help find your husband. But I need to ask you some questions first."

Melissa nodded and sat up straighter. Wiping the tears away with the sleeve of her shirt, she asked, "What do you need to know?"

"Rose Sherman." Cassie didn't hesitate. They had to find out more about the woman. "Tell me everything."

24

Harris hoped Cassie was having better luck. Considering Robert's wife hadn't barged in on her yet, things seemed to be going well out there. Or maybe Mrs. Sherman had called the cops and Harris was about to get arrested and sent back to Savannah with her tail between her legs.

But she didn't have time to worry about that right now. She'd found Robert Sherman's office—a moderately styled room lined with bookshelves and dotted with plush chairs. In its center sat a solid, shiny, dark wooden desk. It looked expensive, but she could barely see it under all the paperwork scattered across its surface. Something told her that when guests came over, this room was off limits.

Harris approached the desk, spotting a closed laptop under a book and a pile of papers. Brushing them to the side, she accidentally knocked the book off the desk in the process. But it didn't matter. If Robert Sherman was in trouble, he wouldn't mind her ransacking his desk if it meant saving his ass.

The laptop was password protected. It was up for debate if Robert was smart enough not to write the information down somewhere, but even if he wasn't, there was no telling where he would've kept it. Harris took a deep breath before digging in.

She opened the drawers one at a time, looking for something—anything. Whether it was the password or something more significant didn't matter. She didn't know what she was after, but she'd recognize it when she found it.

What she found was a whole lot of nothing. Pens and pencils. Blank computer paper. All the office supplies you'd expect and nothing you wouldn't. It seemed painfully ordinary, much to her annoyance. Even the hanging files related to his job appeared unimportant. Scanning the names of the accounts on the tabs, nothing stuck out. None matched the companies associated with the sleazy lawyer, Reed. She knew it was all related somehow, otherwise she wouldn't be here. But it felt like they were attacking the same problem from two different angles and never meeting in the middle.

Harris slammed the last drawer shut and growled in frustration. Time felt like it was slipping through her fingers, no matter how tightly she gripped it. If Cassie were here, she'd make some reference to that Salvador Dalí painting where the clocks hung limply from tree branches, like they were about to drip into oblivion. Every step forward had been a lucky stumble. And she couldn't guarantee she'd find the answers she was looking for.

She had to wonder if she really wanted the answers after all.

Cassie had tried to warn her. David hadn't wanted them looking into his death, and Harris had ignored those wishes without a second thought. She didn't regret her choice. She refused to feel guilty. How could he ask that of her? He was gone, and she was left to pick up the pieces. He didn't get to decide how she mourned him. How she would put her own life back together.

Then there was the spreadsheet. Seeing that date had triggered an avalanche of memories. Moments she had worked tirelessly to erase from her consciousness. Cassie had seen her surprise, and instead of opening up to her friend, Harris had shut her out. But she had more important problems to solve now.

Like figuring out where the hell Rose Sherman was hiding.

Harris stood and looked at the bookshelves. They were a mess. Each shelf was double stacked, with books shoved in wherever there was room. Little knickknacks were hidden here and there, including a crocheted banker. Harris wondered if Robert's wife had made it herself. She walked around the desk to take a closer look at the tomes he'd put on display. What did Robert Sherman like reading?

It turned out he was a fan of everything. From books on investing and the stock market, to *Paradise Lost* and *Of Mice and Men*. He even had the *Harry Potter* series and *The Hunger Games*. Harris wondered if this was the family library, or if Robert was really that eclectic of a reader.

Not that it mattered. The answer wouldn't help her find what she was looking for.

Harris turned back to the desk, certain she had missed something. She stopped dead when she spotted the book she'd knocked over earlier. It was the only one that hadn't been shoved onto the shelf with the others.

Stooping to pick it up, she wondered what significance it could have. When she flipped it over, it took her a second to take in the title. *Moby Dick*. Her least favorite book in the entire world. She had been forced to read every excruciating page in high school. Talk about bad memories.

She almost tossed it aside in disgust.

Then she thought better of it. Harris allowed the little hardcover to flip open to a random page in her palm. Inside, there was a picture and a stack of receipts. Her heart thumped, and she drew the book closer to get a better look.

The picture was an old polaroid from the eighties, colored sepia from age. The two young men were barely adults, with wispy mustaches and shorts that showed off their scrawny thighs. They had their arms thrown around each other's shoulders, each holding up a can of Coke in salute to the photographer. They looked happy.

Underneath was another photo. This one had been printed from a film camera. Someone had coerced the two men into replicating the polaroid. They were older by about ten or fifteen years, and each had a *let's get this over with* grin on their face. This time, they held up two beers in salute. It wasn't hard to tell who it was this time.

On the left, Randall Sherman. He wore a polo shirt and a pair of khakis with his belt tied a little too tight. The smile didn't reach his eyes, whether from the booze or life tearing him down one day at a time, she couldn't tell. Either way, she recognized him instantly. The man who had started all of this. The man whose murder she'd witnessed.

On the right was Robert Sherman. He looked a little older than his cousin, but much happier. He wore a dress shirt and slacks. His belt a perfect fit. His grin was wide, like he was hamming it up for the camera. There was laughter in his eyes, and you could tell he was having a great time. Maybe it was the beer or life building him up one day at a time.

Harris looked up, not seeing the room around her, but lost in thought. Robert had two pictures of him and his cousin tucked away in a book, presumably where no one—including his wife—could find them. Was Randall the dirty little secret of the family? If so, it looked like Robert hadn't forgotten the good times they'd spent together. And if he was holding onto these memories, Rose might've felt comfortable reaching out to Robert if she was in trouble.

Harris looked back down at the book and pulled the pictures and the stack of receipts out, making sure nothing else was inside before tossing it back on top of the desk. She slipped the photos into her pocket, and then unfolded the receipts. Her heart played a staccato rhythm as they painted a clear picture for her.

The first one was for a restaurant at the Hyatt in downtown Chicago. There were two meals listed—spaghetti and meatballs and chicken marsala. One glass of wine and a water. The total was far more expensive than she would've guessed, and it was paid for with Robert's credit card. A staple in the top right corner had her flipping over the receipt and taking note of the parking validation on the back. Same hotel. The time stamp told her Robert had been there two days prior. Is this where he was now? Had he really forgotten his kid's play?

The other receipt was for the grocery store. There were only a few items, like bread, deli meats, some fruits, and a couple of snacks.

Exactly what someone would need if they were holing up in their hotel room for a few days, not wanting to risk going out to eat or being disturbed by the staff.

The last receipt was from CVS. It was miles long, filled with coupons, but there was only one item listed at the top. Pre-natal vitamins.

Unless the wife was hiding a baby bump for her second kid, this had to be for Rose Sherman.

And Harris now knew where she was staying.

Harris burst from the room, catching Cassie and the other woman mid-conversation. Cassie glowered at her, like Harris had interrupted something important, but what Harris had found couldn't wait. She motioned Cassie toward the door. "We need to go."

The wife stood, wringing her hands in front of her. "What is it? What's wrong? Bob—"

Harris pinned the woman with her gaze. They didn't have time to explain if they wanted to catch up with Robert and Rose, but she didn't want Robert's wife calling the cops, either. They would just get in the way. "I think I know where your husband is. But we need to leave now. As soon as we find him, we'll have him call you, okay?"

The woman looked to Cassie, who put a gentle hand on her shoulder. "You can trust her."

The wife looked scared and lost and confused, but she pursed her lips and nodded. "Please hurry."

Harris didn't need any more permission than that. Without saying another word, she crossed the room and yanked the front door open, stalking back toward the rental. She heard Cassie scrambling to keep up, but it was a distant sound. Too many possibilities filled her head.

Whether she wanted them or not, the answers she desperately needed were now within reach.

25

CASSIE HAD TO SCRAMBLE OUT OF THE CAR TO KEEP UP WITH HARRIS. By the time she caught up, she was out of breath. "Where's the fire?"

"We're close to something. I can feel it." The detective pushed through the revolving door of the Hyatt. She had to wait for Cassie to catch up. "The wife knows something. I know she does."

As soon as Harris had produced the receipts for the hotel, they had wasted no time. Cassie hadn't even had a chance to tell her everything she had learned from Melissa Sherman. And they had no plan. Which usually didn't bode well.

Harris stood in the middle of the grand lobby, decorated in red and white for the holiday season, ignoring the woman behind the check-in desk, until she spotted the entrance to the bar and restaurant.

Cassie waved an apologetic hand at the concierge before following Harris. The restaurant was dimly lit, giving it an air of quiet elegance. All the lighting was low and golden, allowing just enough illumination to read the menu in the first place. If people couldn't read the prices, maybe they'd order more drinks.

A young blonde woman with perfect porcelain skin stood behind a podium with a wide smile on her face that didn't reach her eyes. "Hello!" She had a slight southern drawl. "Two today?"

"Three, actually. We're here to meet our friend. Have you seen her? She's very pregnant."

"Oh." The woman took in the information without ever dropping her smile. Cassie had the urge to hide her face. "I don't think I have yet, sorry."

"That's okay." Harris pointed behind the woman. "We can wait at the bar?"

"Oh. Um, sure."

"Great. Thank you."

Harris moved past the woman, and Cassie scrambled to catch up. "Waiting for a pregnant woman at a bar? We could have just taken a seat."

"Then we'd have to order something. I don't know about you, but this isn't my usual scene."

That's true. Harris looked like she'd fit in better at a biker bar. And Cassie looked like she primarily spent her time in coffee shops, ordering lattes and reading books. "Okay, but if the hostess hasn't seen Rose—"

"She's not the only person who works here." Harris sat down at a barstool and patted the one next to her. Once Cassie perched on its edge, Harris nodded her head in approval. "Trust me, we'll figure this out. She's close. I know she is."

Cassie was less confident. Even though the receipt was only a couple days old, Rose could've moved on by now. Maybe Bob had set her up in a different hotel room. Maybe Chicago had been a pit stop before she moved on to somewhere else. If she was smart, that's what she should've done.

Before Cassie could voice her worry, a young man emerged from the back, carrying a small box with the word *cocktail straws* stamped along one side. He had blonde hair and tanned skin, both of which looked like the result of hours in the sun. In fact, the kid would've fit in better at a beach bar in California.

A few other patrons dotted the bar, but most were sitting down in booths. Even so, it took the kid a few minutes to spot them, and when he did, he looked startled, like they'd appeared out of nowhere. He jogged over with a huge smile on his face.

"Sorry, ladies. Didn't see you there." He even had the slow, easy-going drawl of someone who had grown up on the West Coast. "What can I get you?"

"Actually, we're waiting on a friend," Harris said.

"Yeah? Maybe I can keep you company for a while."

"Don't you have work to do?"

"I'm a great multi-tasker."

"I bet you are." Harris laughed, and Cassie fought the urge to gape at her. She'd never heard the detective flirt before, and there was something strange about it. Maybe because she knew Harris well enough to know all she wanted was information about Rose. "Can we each get a rum and Coke, please?" Harris continued. "Then maybe we can chat."

"Two rum and Cokes, coming right up."

Cassie leaned over to her friend. "What are you doing?" she hissed.

"Reading the room," Harris hissed back. "Just play along."

The bartender returned with their drinks a few seconds later. Cassie took a sip and almost spit it back out. It tasted like he'd filled the entire glass with rum and added a drop of Coke on top for flavor. She was all for getting her money's worth, but it had to be drinkable.

Harris didn't seem to notice. Taking a huge sip, she smiled. The bartender beamed back at her, and Cassie noticed for the first time how huge his pupils were. Was he high? She took a subtle whiff of the air but didn't smell anything.

"What's your name?" Harris asked.

"Charlie."

"Hi, Charlie. I'm Addie." She held out her hand so he could shake it. "And this is my friend Cassie."

Cassie shook his hand, which was warm and sweaty. "Hello."

"Charlie," Harris said, drawing the man's attention back to her, "we're looking for a friend of ours. Do you think you could help us?"

It looked like he wanted nothing more than to do exactly that. "Yeah, I can help."

"Great!" Harris kept the smile plastered on her face, never dropping eye contact. "She's really, really pregnant. Like, eight months pregnant. Have you seen anyone like that around here?"

"Not that I can think of." He frowned. "Don't get a lot of pregnant women at the bar."

"That's true, but what about the dining area? Have you seen anyone here in the last day or two?"

"No, sorry. I don't really pay much attention unless they're at the bar."

Harris frowned. "That's too bad." She lit up a second later. "Hey, I have an idea." She pointed to the computer that acted like a register. "You charge drinks to people's rooms, right?"

"Yeah, sure."

"Well, can you look up someone's room from there?"

"Yeah. I just need their name."

"Would you do that for us, Charlie? Could you look up our friend so we know which room she's staying in?"

"Oh." For the first time, Charlie's smile faltered. He looked a little scared now. "I'm sorry, but I'm not supposed to do that. I could get in trouble."

"Really?" Harris's voice was sweet as sugar. "Even if we promise not to tell?"

"I'm sorry." He took a step back, like it would be easier to say no to her if he just put a little distance between them. "I really can't. I'd be in, like, so much trouble if I got caught."

"Hmm." Harris leaned to one side and stuck her hand in her coat pocket. She brought something out and put it on the counter, keeping her hand covering most of it. But Cassie could tell what it was. And so could Charlie. A badge. "What about now?"

Charlie was staring down at the badge, panic in his eyes. He couldn't take his eyes off it. "What?"

"Charlie, look at me." She only continued when he pulled his gaze away from the badge and met her eyes. "Come here." She crooked a finger, and he closed the distance between them. "You've got a little something here." Harris wiped at her nose.

Charlie's eyes went wide, and he wiped his nose with the back of his hand. Then realized his mistake. "Please. I need this job."

"Look, Charlie. I'm not here for you. Your boss never has to know what you do in the back room on your breaks." Harris made sure she had Charlie's full attention before she continued. "But my friend is in trouble. I need to know if she's still here. And I need to know what room she's staying in. If you can tell me that, I'll leave. And you can go about your evening."

"O-Okay."

"Good. Her name is Rose Sherman."

Charlie didn't hesitate. Turning to the computer, he tapped in the name. A second later, he looked back up at them. His eyes were even wider than before. "There's no one here staying under that name."

"Shit." Harris looked at Cassie. "I didn't think she'd leave so soon."

"Try Rose Weismann." Cassie leaned over to Harris while Charlie typed it in. "Her maiden name. I asked Melissa in case she started using alternate accounts or something."

"Smart girl." Harris smiled at her. "You sure you don't want to be a cop?"

Cassie blushed at the compliment but shook her head.

"She's staying in room 1075." Charlie was practically in tears. "Please don't tell my boss."

"I won't." Harris stood and leaned over the bar. "But you'll get caught sooner or later. You can do better than this."

Charlie nodded his head vigorously until Harris and Cassie left the bar and headed for the elevators. Only when they were inside, alone, and racing toward the tenth floor, did Cassie turn to Harris and ask, "Where did you get the badge?"

"Oh, this?" She held it out for Cassie. "It's fake."

"Fake?"

"Fake." The detective laughed. "I'm suspended, remember?

Bought it at a costume shop before I came here. Figured it'd come in handy."

"What if someone calls your bluff?"

"I wasn't about to use it on someone who knew better. Charlie wasn't calling anyone's bluff."

"Fair enough."

The elevator *dinged*, and the two got off, quickly finding the signs that pointed them to room 1075.

Rose's room was far from the elevators, and Cassie wondered how much Bob had thought this plan through. If she was eight months pregnant, she wouldn't be able to escape quickly. But maybe he'd been banking on the fact that she'd be able to hide under her maiden name.

Cassie saw Harris stiffen ahead of her. "What's wrong?"

The detective didn't answer. Pulling out her gun, she turned to Cassie, holding a finger to her lips.

Cassie looked around the other woman and noticed what had set her off. The door was wide open, and even from here, she could see someone had ransacked the place. Her stomach clenched in fear, and she prayed they weren't too late.

26

"Stay here," Harris hissed. She brought her gun up and pointed at the room. "Until I say it's clear. Okay?"

Cassie couldn't make a sound. Her heart pounded, and worst-case scenarios were running through her head like a flipbook. Had Aguilar's men found Rose's room? Would she be inside, injured or worse? What if they'd taken her? How had no one noticed the open door?

When Harris turned back to Cassie to confirm she'd been heard, Cassie nodded and watched as the detective entered the room. Harris was as quiet as a mouse, first clearing the bathroom on the left, then the small closet on the right. Both flinched when the hinge squeaked, but the detective had one eye on the rest of the room the entire time.

After ensuring no one was hiding behind the door either, Harris entered the larger area containing one queen-sized bed and a chair. She lifted the skirt on the bed, but even from the hallway, Cassie could see no one would be able to fit under there.

"Okay, it's clear," Harris called out.

Cassie took a tentative step inside. The bathroom light was on, which made it easier to see the mess someone had made. Towels were strewn across the floor, and the shower curtain had been half torn from the rod. Sample sizes of soap and shampoo had been knocked over, the contents spilling across the tile.

The rest of the room was worse. The comforter and sheets were in a pile on the floor, and the chair for the desk had been knocked over. Whoever had done this had also smashed the coffee pot against the wall. Pieces of plastic and glass littered the floor.

"There's a bag over here." Harris knelt. She still hadn't put her gun away, but she kept it aimed at the floor. "Looks like they went through it, too. Just a bunch of clothes. They all look new."

"Bob must've bought them for her. Or gave her money for them."

"Bob?"

"Robert." Cassie felt like she was in a haze. "Melissa kept calling him Bob. I think that's what he goes by."

"Oh."

It was such an unimportant detail, but amid everything else, Cassie felt like Harris should know. Bob was missing, and now so was Rose. Aguilar's men had tracked them to Chicago, trying to clean up the mess Randall had started. They were close enough to get to Harris and Cassie, too. She felt exposed. Vulnerable.

"Adelaide, I think we should leave."

"Not yet." Harris was sifting through the pile of sheets. "I want to make sure we're not missing anything."

Cassie swallowed her fear, feeling it settle in her stomach like a rock. "It looks like they were searching for something."

"The flash drive, maybe? Or something else." Harris stood up and looked around. "They must think Rose has something on Aguilar. This isn't just about making sure she doesn't know anything. This is about making sure she isn't planning to tell anyone."

"We have no idea where they could've taken her." Cassie's breaths were ragged. "She could be anywhere. She could already be—"

"Hang on, hang on." Harris tucked her gun away and walked up to Cassie, placing a reassuring hand on her arm. "There's no blood here. That's a good sign. It means she either wasn't here to begin with, or they took her somewhere else."

"How is that a good thing?"

"If they do have her, they're not going to kill her right away. They want something from her. We have a chance to get her back."

Cassie opened her mouth to say that wasn't exactly ideal when she heard a small gasp behind her. Harris's gaze shifted from Cassie's face to the open doorway, and her eyes widened. But before Cassie could turn around, Harris was shoving past her and sprinting out of the room. Without thinking, Cassie took off after her.

The detective was halfway down the hall. It hadn't taken her long to catch up to whoever had appeared outside the door. It wasn't until Harris grabbed the woman's arm and spun her around that Cassie recognized who it was.

Rose Sherman.

She had red hair drawn up into a ponytail. Her face was bare of any makeup, and her eyes were puffy, like she hadn't slept in days. Her outfit consisted of a maternity dress and thick leggings, with a cardigan and puffy jacket on top. By the time Cassie caught up to them, Rose was already screaming.

"Get away from me! Help! Help!"

"Rose! Rose. My name is Adelaide. We're not going to hurt you. We're here to help."

The woman kept screaming. A few doors opened, and a couple of people stuck their heads out.

"Rose, I knew your husband. I knew Randall."

Rose stopped yelling. Tears were tracking down her face. "You knew Randall?"

"Yes. My name is Adelaide Harris, and I—"

"Detective Harris?"

"Yes, I'm Detective Harris. Did he tell you about me?"

She nodded her head. "You worked with Detective Klein."

"That's right."

Rose looked past Harris. "Who are you?"

"I'm Cassie." She stepped forward. "I didn't know your husband, but I was friends with David. Um, Detective Klein."

A big man with curly hair stepped out into the hallway with just a robe on. "Is everything okay out here? Ma'am, do you need help?"

"No, I'm okay. I'm sorry." Rose seemed to take in the hallway of onlookers for the first time. She raised her voice a little. "Sorry. It was just a misunderstanding. I'm okay. Thank you."

A few people grumbled and went back inside their rooms. But a couple of the nosier ones kept watching. Harris gently tugged on the sleeve of Rose's jacket. "Come on, let's go back to your room."

"Is it safe?"

"It's safe. No one's in there."

Rose gulped but followed Harris and Cassie back to her room. When she stepped inside, she looked around in horror. "They found me."

"Who did?"

"Aguilar's men. How did they find me?"

"We'll figure that out later," Harris said. "For now, I think it's best you come with us."

"Where?" Her eyes grew wide. "Please don't take me back to Savannah. The police, he's got them on his payroll. They'll kill me."

"We're not taking you back to Savannah." Cassie stepped forward. She wanted to hug Rose but wasn't sure how the other woman would react. "You can stay with us. In our hotel room."

"Rose, they were looking for something," Harris said. "Did you have any evidence on you? Something Randall gave you?"

The woman shook her head. "I didn't have time to pack a bag or anything. Bob gave me some money for clothes." Harris and Cassie exchanged a look at the mention of the cousin. "What? What is it? Is Bob okay?"

"We think someone took him." Harris's voice was gentle, but there was no real way to sugarcoat information like that.

"Took him? Where? Who?"

"Might be the same people who did this." Harris gestured around the room. "Either way, we should move. You can pack up your stuff, and we'll take you back to our hotel. Then we'll figure out what to do from there."

Rose looked like she was ready to pass out, either from exhaustion or stress or some combination of the two. Still, she pressed her lips together and nodded her head, then gathered her belongings in the duffel bag. Harris took it from her and shouldered it, leading the way out of the room.

Cassie wanted to offer the other woman some words of encouragement, but she knew there was nothing she could say to make her feel any better.

27

Rose entered their hotel room sandwiched between Harris and Cassie. Part of Cassie was worried Rose would bolt at the first available opportunity but reminded herself the woman had nowhere to go. Her best option was to shack up with a couple of complete strangers.

"You can take Cassie's bed," Harris said. "She can sleep with me. Or I can sleep on the floor."

"We can share. It's not a problem." They all needed as much rest as possible. "Do you need anything else, Rose? More clothes or vitamins?"

"Food?" Harris offered. "There's room service. Or one of us could run to the store."

Rose had been peeking out through the curtains, watching the road below. When she turned around, her eyes were still wide with fear. "No, I'm okay." When Harris and Cassie leveled her with a look, she sat down on the bed. "Really, I'm okay. I was just out getting something to eat. That's why I wasn't in my room. Lucky, I guess."

"Very lucky." Harris shrugged out of her jacket. She took a seat on the bed opposite Rose. "I really need to ask you some questions about this whole situation. Are you up for that?"

Rose took a deep breath and blew it out. Face pinched in pain, she grabbed her belly. After shifting around for a second, she looked over at Harris. "I'll do my best. I don't know everything. Randall didn't want me getting mixed up in any of this. But he also couldn't lie to me." The smile on her face was sad. "I always got it out of him eventually." The smile faded, and she looked down at her feet. "Kind of regret that now."

"Everything Randall did was for you," Harris said. "He loved you very much."

"Thanks." Rose looked exhausted but met Harris's eyes. "What do you need to know?"

"Do you have any idea how this all started? How your husband got mixed up with Aguilar?"

"Not really. Randall was always smart. Always good with numbers. But bad at keeping jobs. Kind of a space cadet, you know? Had trouble concentrating, and when he did concentrate, it was usually on the wrong thing. He'd find the most interesting project instead of the most important one." Rose took a deep breath and shifted on the bed again. "One day, he came home and said he lost his job. This was quite a few years ago. And not the first time it had happened. Neither one of us made a lot of money, so I was scared. Said some things I shouldn't have. He left. When he came back, he said he fixed it."

"Fixed it?" Harris raised an eyebrow. "How?"

"I don't know. He said he got a job as a freelance accountant. I'm horrible with numbers." Rose laughed, but it didn't reach her eyes. "I don't even know if that's a real thing. I couldn't understand his job if someone held a gun to my head." Pausing, as though realizing that was a very real scenario for her now. "But I guess I didn't care. Once he started making money, we tucked it away as often as we could. We didn't want to have kids without something in our savings account."

"When did you think something else was going on?"

"There wasn't a single moment. Looking back now, I can see all sorts of signs. He was usually paid in cash. Sometimes he'd come home with presents. Like a diamond necklace. I told him not to spend our money on that, but he said he didn't. That it was a present from his employer. I thought it was weird, but I liked being spoiled."

"Well, I probably wouldn't have refused it either," Harris said. Cassie could tell the detective had said that to reassure the other woman, but it seemed to work. The slope of Rose's shoulders relaxed a little.

"More and more money started coming in. I was happy about it, obviously. But something just didn't sit right with me. Randall kept saying it was because there were more clients. Later I found out he only had one client—Aguilar."

"How was he getting more money then?" Cassie asked.

"Aguilar was acquiring more businesses. As he came to trust Randall, he brought him into more of his prospects. Had him doing the books for a bunch of his investments." She shook her head. "I didn't know that until later. When we had to move."

"You had to move?" Harris asked. "Why?"

"It wasn't safe anymore. This was a few years ago still, but Aguilar had made enemies with someone powerful. I don't know who, but he started going after Aguilar's people. Someone broke into our house when we were gone. Aguilar bought us a new home. Moved us closer to him. Randall had no choice but to tell me who his boss was."

"And Randall knew what Aguilar was into," Harris said. There was an unasked question in her tone.

Rose sighed. "Yes. Look, Randall was a good person, but he was impulsive. He was scared I was going to leave him, so he took a job with Aguilar. I don't know how he even knew him in the first place. Maybe the guy had met Randall somewhere and offered him a job that he'd refused. Anyway, he went back to Aguilar and agreed to work for him. He knew Aguilar was shady, but I don't think he had any idea what he was really into. If he did, he wouldn't have agreed to it. I know he wouldn't."

"I don't think so either," Harris said. "I met Randall once. He cared about you. About his family. He knew it was a bad idea to cross Aguilar, but he did it because it was the right thing to do."

"And look where it got him."

"The best thing we can do is make sure Aguilar doesn't hurt anyone else." Harris hesitated, and Cassie could tell she was weighing her words. Rose was opening up to them, but still looked ready to bolt. "What else did Randall tell you?"

"Little things. Times where he'd figure out Aguilar was moving some big shipment or something. When he got paid a lot of money, it was hard to say no. We really wanted kids. And we wanted them better off than we were." She rubbed her stomach absentmindedly. "But he got scared. He wouldn't tell me, but I think Aguilar made him keep track of other things. Bad things. That's when Randall decided he'd had enough."

"What happened?"

"We talked about it for a while. He knew Aguilar had people in the police department working for him. But there was one guy who was different from the others. He didn't want to be there. Like he was being blackmailed or something. Randall sent him anonymous letters at first. And once he decided he could trust the guy, they began working together."

"Who was it? The cop?"

Rose looked confused for a second. "Detective Klein. Didn't you know he was working with Aguilar?"

Harris stood up, and Cassie jumped. "David wasn't undercover for Aguilar."

"Not undercover." Rose glanced at the door, like she was gauging how far away it was in case she had to escape. "He was working *for* him. I think he was paying down some sort of debt."

"A debt?" Harris's entire body went stiff. "What kind of debt?"

"I don't know. All Randall told me was that Detective Klein had asked Aguilar for a favor. He spent years paying it off."

"Years?"

"Yeah."

Harris looked like she was going to be sick. "Do you have any idea—I mean, do you know when David asked for this favor?"

"Not exactly." Rose glanced between Harris and Cassie, looking just as confused as Cassie felt. "But definitely several years ago.

Randall had known about Detective Klein for a while before he reached out."

"Adelaide." Cassie couldn't keep the warble out of her voice. "What's going on?"

"It's all my fault." Harris looked close to crying. "That deal David made with Aguilar." She looked up, and Cassie had to blink back her own tears. She'd never seen such sadness in the detective's eyes. "I think it's because of something I did."

28

Zbirak stood back along the wall, careful not to lean against it. The basement he had acquired for this job was not the cleanest, and he wished to keep up his own appearances. It would be difficult to spot residue on the black button-down shirt and slacks he'd recently purchased, but he would know it was there. And that was enough.

The room was small. Cramped. There was a hint of mildew in the air, covered by the searing scent of bleach and the putrid stench of something else. He glared at Mr. Thompson for the third or fourth time that evening. When he'd told Mr. Thompson to clean the room, Zbirak thought the man would hire a legitimate cleaning crew. It never occurred to him Thompson would simply pour bleach on the floor and wipe it around for a few minutes.

What was the point in cleaning for their guest if this was the result?

Zbirak turned his attention back to Robert Sherman. Or Bob, as he preferred. What a congenial, utterly boring name. *Bob*. It didn't feel right coming out of his mouth. It felt too simple, too plebian. He'd call him Mr. Sherman. It was decided.

Zbirak stepped forward. "Mr. Sherman, I hate to be so heavy-handed. I hope you know that."

Sherman flinched, but otherwise did not respond. He was tied to a chair made from cherry wood. Zbirak had seen it in an antique store and couldn't resist its charm. Of course, he hadn't intended to use it during an interrogation, but he enjoyed putting it to good use. He had warned Thompson not to damage it, but that was likely a lost cause. Thompson didn't have the lightest of touches.

"But time is of the essence here. I need answers."

"I told you everything." Mr. Sherman's voice was husky from yelling. "Please. I don't know anything else."

"I don't like being lied to."

Sherman finally looked up. For the first time since he'd returned, Zbirak saw the extent of the man's injuries. Thompson had concentrated his blows on the man's face, giving him two black eyes and a split lip. Blood trickled from his nose, but it didn't look broken. Zbirak had instructed Thompson to rough the man up, but he didn't want to leave him with any lasting injuries. Not yet.

"I'm not lying." Sherman wept. "Please."

"Let's go over what we know so far, shall we? Just in case you're feeling a little behind the rest of the class." Zbirak paced back and forth, ticking items off his fingers. "Rose contacted you because you are Randall's cousin. She trusted you because you and Randall used to run in similar circles before you got a corporate job, though you weren't above helping him out once in a while for a little extra cash. Georgie needs to go to a good college, right?" He paused to level a look at Sherman before continuing. "You put Rose up in a hotel room for a few days. However, when Thompson went to check, she wasn't there. We're left with one of two options. You either lied about the room number, or you somehow warned her ahead of time. As you've been here without your phone for the last two hours, I suspect it's the first option."

"Please. I didn't lie. I swear I told you the truth. Room 1075. At the Hyatt Regency. That's where I left her."

Thompson emerged from the shadows with a growl in his voice. "You calling *me* a liar?"

Sherman flinched again. "No. No. I'm just s-saying. S-She was there. That w-was her room number."

"Mr. Thompson, let's go over the details of your investigation again, just so Mr. Sherman is on the same page."

Thompson turned toward Zbirak with a sneer. The man always sneered. He had the blackest eyes Zbirak had ever seen, like a shark who smelled blood in the water. Where Zbirak was tall and lean, Thompson was short and stocky. Zbirak did not fear the man, but he had no interest in tangling with him. There was no doubt in Zbirak's mind that he'd win, but Thompson would land some heavy punches along the way. It was best to keep the man happy. Or as happy as someone like him could be.

"Mr. Thompson," Zbirak started. "You went to Rose Sherman's room? Number 1075?"

"Yes," Thompson replied.

"And what did you find inside?"

"Nothing."

"Not a single person?"

"No."

"Any belongings, or was the room empty and clean?"

"A duffel bag. Women's clothing."

Sherman's head snapped up. "See? It was her room. P-please—"

"But no indication that the clothes belonged to Rose Sherman?" Zbirak continued, as though he hadn't been interrupted.

"None." The growl in Thompson's voice was sadistic, as though he looked forward to what came next.

And how could Zbirak deny him what he wanted?

"Mr. Sherman, it seems we do not have proof enough that you've given us the correct information. We need more from you."

"I don't know anything else. Please." He looked up at Zbirak with pleading eyes. "Please, I'll do anything. Money? Whatever your boss is paying you, I'll double it. Triple it."

"You couldn't afford me." It was Zbirak's turn to sneer now. He hated when his guests turned into sniveling beggars. Didn't anyone have a backbone anymore? "No, I need more information."

"I've told you everything!" Sherman roared, rocking back and forth in the chair, struggling against his bonds. He tipped to the left, and then too far to the right. Gravity took him to the floor, and he landed with a grunt.

Zbirak forced himself not to wince. The chair didn't look broken, but he was out of patience. "Mr. Thompson, please pick him up." Zbirak waited until it was done. "Mr. Sherman, if you do that again, I will be forced to cut a limb from your body." Was it overkill? Perhaps. But he was fond of that chair, and the man needed to know that Zbirak was serious. "If you will not cooperate of your own volition, I'll hand the reins over to Mr. Thompson."

That's all Thompson needed to hear. He stepped forward, reared back, and slammed his fist into Sherman's nose. There was a crunch and a cry of pain before blood exploded from his face. Thompson looked down in satisfaction before pulling out a rag from his back pocket and wiping his knuckles clean.

"Look at that." Thompson pointed to a mermaid tattoo on his arm. "You made a mess of Betsy. You'll pay for that."

Betsy? Zbirak rolled his eyes. A stupid name for a stupid tattoo. But he wouldn't interrupt the other man's work. Whatever mind games Thompson wanted to play were fine with Zbirak. As long as it got him results. But he wouldn't stand idly by.

"If you won't talk, Mr. Sherman, then I'll find another way to get the information I want. I believe your wife is still at home, awaiting your return. With little Georgie by her side. Something tells me she'll be more than cooperative."

"Wait! Wait!" Sherman got the words out before Zbirak even had time to turn around and head toward the exit. "Please don't hurt them. This is between you and me."

"No, Mr. Sherman. This is between me and Rose. You are merely a means to an end. As is the rest of your family."

"I have her phone number." Sherman hung his head in defeat. "We bought it for emergencies. She won't answer for anyone but me."

"Ah, Mr. Sherman." Zbirak smiled. This was good news, indeed. "I knew you were holding out on me."

29

CASSIE HELD HER BREATH, WAITING FOR HARRIS TO SAY SOMETHING.
Harris stared off into space, as though reliving the worst days of her
life. Rose shifted uncomfortably on the bed, breaking the spell.
Cassie took a step forward.

"Adelaide, what are you—"

Harris stood. "I don't want to talk about it."

"Tell me what's going on."

"Stay out of it, Cassie. You can't fix this."

"I'm not trying to *fix* anything." The anger and sadness that had
been building inside burst from her chest. There was a growl in her
voice, and she took Harris by the shoulders. "I lost David, too,
Adelaide. And I want and deserve to know why. I knew that man for
ten years. He was my best friend. The only person I could go to when
shit got hard. I can't live the rest of my life thinking he was paid off by
Aguilar. There's got to be another reason. Some explanation for why
he'd do that."

Harris looked at Cassie, and for a moment, she thought the detective was going to snap back. Instead, she deflated in her arms, sagged
back down onto the bed, and put her face in her hands. "I don't know
everything."

"I don't need to know everything. Just what's weighing on you. Maybe I can't change anything, but you won't have to deal with this all on your own."

Harris groaned and looked up at Cassie. Something in her eyes seemed wild and unhinged. Desperate. But blinking it away, she was Adelaide again. "At the beginning of my career, I fired my gun and killed someone. A nineteen-year-old kid. The situation was complicated."

Cassie kept her voice gentle. Encouraging. "Complicated?"

"I caught him trying to rob a convenience store after hours. Later I found out his dad owned the store. Someone had called it in, though, and I responded." She took a deep breath. "He was aggressive, high on something, and ranting and raving. When he pulled a knife, I pulled my gun. It was just meant to be a warning. Hell, I didn't even have it raised. Then he charged." Lifting her sleeve, she showed Cassie a thin white scar on her arm where she'd blocked a blow. "I managed to get him off, but he raised the knife again. I panicked and fired."

"You were defending yourself."

Harris shook her head. "Doesn't matter. I should've found another way." The detective looked up at Cassie like she wanted the woman to hate her. "He had a knife. I had a gun."

"But he was still dangerous." Cassie knelt in front of Harris. "What if he took your gun, or stabbed you. You were protecting yourself."

"He was nineteen." A sob escaped, but Harris was quick to pull it back. "With his whole life ahead of him. He could've turned things around, but I took that from him."

There was nothing Cassie could say to make her feel better, but that didn't mean she wouldn't try. "You were cleared to go back to active duty, right? They would've investigated. You're still a detective."

Harris shrugged. "He had a record. He came from a family of criminals. His father was Luca White, one of the biggest drug traffickers in Savannah. No one felt bad about his death. Except me. And David. He knew how I felt. He understood how hard it was."

"Why do you think this had something to do with David and Aguilar?"

Harris re-centered herself, her voice steadier now. "White went on a rampage after this. He was gunning for me. Half the force kept detail on my house for a month. It wasn't a good time for me." She rubbed the scar on her arm. "David stayed with me the entire time. He said he wouldn't let anything happen to me. That he'd take care of everything."

"I'm assuming they arrested White after that?"

Harris shook her head. "He was sloppy. Not really keeping a low profile. One day, White turned up dead. Shot pointblank. Aguilar filled the vacuum after that. No one can prove it, but I always thought he killed White. Took over his operations." She nodded toward the computer, where the flash drive was. "That first date on David's record was only a few months after I shot White's son."

Cassie tried to keep up, but there were too many puzzle pieces, and she couldn't see how they fit together. "But David wasn't getting paid. It looked like he had a debt with Aguilar."

"You mean like David paying Aguilar to kill White before White had a chance to kill me?"

Cassie shook her head. She didn't want to think about it. "David would never do that." But she didn't feel so sure. White was a bad person. And David would've been trying to save Harris. Cassie looked over at Rose, who had been sitting on the other bed with wide eyes for far too long now. "Do you have any idea? Did Randall ever mention David?"

"I don't know any specifics. I'm sorry." She looked close to tears. "He never said anything other than the bare minimum. He didn't want me—"

A shrill ringtone went off, making all three of them jump.

Harris dug her phone out of her pocket and looked down at it, then up at Cassie and shook her head.

"I'm pretty sure I left mine on vibrate," Cassie said, digging out her own phone and holding it up. The screen was blank.

The two of them turned to Rose, who held a small flip phone. If possible, her eyes were even wider now. When she spoke, there was a tremble in her voice. "It's Bob."

"Put it on speaker," Harris said. Her usual demeanor was back as she strolled across the room. "Don't mention that we're here."

Rose did as she was told. "Hello? Bob?"

"Hey." Bob's voice sounded strained. And the connection was weak. "Where are you?"

"What?"

"Rose, I need to know where you are. You weren't at the hotel room. Where did you go?"

"I went out for dinner. Bob, someone broke in."

"I know. I need to know where you are." There was a pause, a hesitation that told Cassie he was more scared than he was letting on. "I need to know right now."

Rose looked up at Harris, who shook her head. Rose swallowed and a pained expression filled her face. "I don't think I should do that."

Another pause. "Why not?"

"I'm scared. What's going on? Where did you go?"

"I didn't go anywhere. I'm right here. But, Rose, I need you to tell me—"

"They found my hotel room. Did you tell them that?"

There was a small sob, which crackled in the static of the poor connection. "Rose, I—"

Rose looked more resolute now. "I'm not going to tell you where I am."

There was a rustling in the background from the phone exchanging hands. A new voice spoke, louder this time. The call had been taken off speaker. "That's okay, Mrs. Sherman. It won't be long until I find you."

A shiver ran down Cassie's spine. She'd never heard a voice so cold, yet so amused. Harris launched herself from the bed and grabbed the phone from Rose's hand, slamming it shut. Her eyes were wild when she looked at Cassie.

"We need to leave," Harris said. "Now."

30

IT ONLY TOOK THE THREE OF THEM A FEW MINUTES TO GRAB THEIR things. Rose hadn't unpacked her duffel yet, and both Cassie and Harris had been living out of their bags since they got to the hotel room. All Harris had to do was shove the computer into her backpack, and they were ready to leave.

"Do we need to get rid of the phone?" Rose asked, scrambling after them.

Cassie jogged to keep up with the detective. "And who was the other man on the phone?"

Harris opened the flip phone and hit a few buttons. "We're keeping the phone, but I'm turning it off for now." She ran up to the elevator and hit the down button. "And I don't know who that was, but I didn't like the sound of his voice."

"Me neither." Rose was shaking. "D-do you think—I mean, what about Bob? Is he gonna be okay?"

Harris waited until all three of them were in the elevator before responding. "I can't make any promises about Bob." Harris turned to Rose and took her bag. "Are you doing okay? Can you keep up?"

Rose had a determined look on her face. "I can keep up."

"Okay. Let's try to get ahead of this thing." The doors to the elevator *dinged* open, and Harris checked the lobby before she allowed the other two off after her. They headed straight for the car. "Rose, I want you in the back seat. Stay down as much as you can, but don't make yourself uncomfortable, okay? Unless he was close by, we've got plenty of time. I just don't want to take any risks."

"Okay."

Harris unlocked the car and tossed their bags in the back. "Cassie, I want you up front. Look for a hotel on the other side of the city. Somewhere nice, with a parking garage."

Cassie slid into the front seat. "Got it. Anything else?"

"You still have that folder?"

It took Cassie a second to remember what the detective was talking about. "From the warehouse? Yeah."

Harris looked over her shoulder at Rose. "Do you know anyone named Don Reed?"

"Don Reed?" Rose sat up a little in the backseat but slunk back down when Harris pulled away from the curve. "Yeah. How do you know him?"

"How do *you* know him?" Harris had one eye on the road, one eye on her rearview.

"Randall mentioned him a few times. I've never met him, but he sounds like a sleazebag. He was always trying to cozy up to Randall."

"Cozy up to him? Why?"

"Either to cover up some mistake he made, or to get something on Randall to take the heat off himself."

"But Randall was smarter than that," Harris said. It wasn't a question.

"Aguilar is a scary guy. Not saying Don Reed isn't, but there's a hierarchy, you know? Aguilar's at the top."

As Cassie waited for a page to load on her phone, she looked back down at the folder in her lap. "We found Reed through a company called Annex, LLC. We don't have a direct tie from Reed to Aguilar, but we think Aguilar has some hand in the business."

"I've definitely heard that company name before." Rose thought for a moment. "Is it some sort of real estate company?"

Harris and Cassie exchanged a look. Harris spoke first. "Yeah. Do you know anything else about it?"

"Not off the top of my head. But I do know Aguilar has a bunch of them. Real estate is one of his more legitimate businesses. A lot of them are just masks to hide the real shady shit he's doing."

Cassie's mind was spinning. It was hard to keep track of all the pieces. And she was still thinking about Harris' situation. Had David really done something to keep her out of trouble? She couldn't imagine David working side by side with someone like Aguilar. Then again, he'd do anything to keep his loved ones safe.

But she had to focus on one thing at a time. "What about Reed?" Cassie asked Rose. "What else do you know about him?"

"Not much. Randall mentioned him a bunch, but he always tried to keep me out of it. Sometimes I overheard him on the phone. But I can't remember anything else. I'm sorry."

"That's okay." Cassie hit another button on her phone. "I've almost got a room picked out."

"Good. What—" Harris broke off, and Cassie looked up to see her squinting in the rearview mirror.

"What's wrong?"

"This guy's riding my ass."

"Might be nothing."

"Might be." Harris didn't sound convinced. She pressed the gas a little harder, and the engine revved as it worked to keep up. "Read out what you see in the folder."

Now that they were away from the hotel, Cassie had to use the light of her phone to illuminate the pages inside. It could've waited until they made it to the other hotel, but she had a feeling Harris was trying to distract Rose from whatever was going on behind them. "It's a bunch of insurance claims. Some are for a couple hundred dollars. Some are for half a million."

"Insurance fraud." They were on Lake Shore Drive now, heading south. Traffic was tight, and Harris used the opportunity to slip in between two other cars before she spoke again. "Annex and all the shell corporations? They're trying to hide that it's all going back to the same person."

"Aguilar?" Rose asked from the back.

Cassie resisted the urge to look over her shoulder to see if the car was still following them. Somehow, that would make it all worse. "Some of these are for Savannah properties. Interesting that Reed would have them, considering his office is in Chicago."

Harris grinned. "That ties Reed to Savannah. Which is one step closer to—"

"Aguilar," Rose and Cassie said in unison.

"Do you recognize any of the addresses?" Harris asked.

"Not really. They have a Savannah zip code, but I don't know what any of them are. I can pull it up on my phone?"

"When we get back to the hotel—" Harris slammed on her brakes, causing both Cassie and Rose to lurch forward, and the folder to dump onto the floor at Cassie's feet. "Shit."

"What? What's wrong?" Cassie couldn't resist the pull now. She looked over her shoulder, only to see a huge Ford F150 filling up the back window. "Is that the guy following us?"

Before Harris could answer, the guy let off his gas and switched lanes. Then exited the highway, leaving them to continue. Harris blew out a breath of air. "Guess not."

"Let's hope it was just a random tailgater and not someone trying to get our license plate," Cassie said, then winced. She didn't want to freak out Rose, but they needed to be honest.

"We'll be careful." Harris's voice was calmer now. "It'll help having the car in a parking garage. Hopefully we're out of here before they manage to track us down."

Cassie leaned forward and scooped the papers off the floor. They were all out of order now. As she tried sorting them in her lap, she came across one that had a sticky note on the back. "Wait a second." She used her phone to illuminate the scribble written there. "There's a list of names here. Johnson. Cleveland." Cassie hesitated. She didn't want to read out the next one. "Klein." She let that sink in, but no one said anything. "Warren."

"Warren?" Harris's voice was deadly serious. "Are you sure?".

"I think so. Why, do you know them?"

"Officer Warren died a week before David. Routine traffic stop. It seemed strange, especially since David died a week later."

"And now Warren's name is in this folder. You think he was investigating this? Maybe he found something on Aguilar."

"Seems more than a little possible. Two people on that list are dead. We need to look into the others."

Silence filled the car. Cassie's head continued to spin, and she didn't know which direction to go in. "What now?"

Harris gripped the steering wheel, keeping her eyes on the road ahead. "We lay low for the night. I'll call in a few favors. We figure out how to keep Rose safe. Then we get some answers."

Cassie had no idea how they were going to do any of those things, but the determination on Harris's face didn't leave any room for doubt.

31

JASON HAD CALLED LATER THAT NIGHT FOR AN UPDATE, AND BY THE NEXT morning, they had figured out how to keep Rose safe. One of Jason's contacts lived just over the border in Wisconsin and ran a security company with a built-in safe house. Jason said his friend wouldn't charge anything to keep Rose holed up for a couple of days, but Cassie couldn't tell if it was because the guy owed Jason a favor, or if Jason was covering the expenses out of his own pocket.

She really hoped it was the former.

But that led to more unanswered questions. How had Jason and this other man met? What had they gone through together? Did the guy know about the part of Jason's past he hadn't felt comfortable sharing with her yet? And what kind of favor constituted a no-questions-asked scenario that involved taking in a stranger?

Unfortunately, she didn't have the time or the energy to ask him what was on her mind. Harris had made all three of them go to bed early that night after having Rose write down everything she could remember about her conversations with her husband. It wasn't much, and the notes were scattered, but they had no idea which details would be important later. Or which might finally nail Aguilar to the wall.

Cassie had to admit she felt better in the morning. The anxiety of being in a foreign city would've been enough to exhaust her, let alone everything else going on. Hitmen and money laundering and shady lawyers. Part of her couldn't wait to get back home to Savannah and a normal life, and part of her knew it would never feel like home without David.

Saying goodbye to Rose was harder than she'd thought it would be. The other woman looked so tiny, despite her pregnant belly, and watching two hulking men standing on either side of her as they got ready to leave only shrunk her further.

Cassie went in for a hug. "You can trust these guys." She kept her voice low, so only Rose could hear her. "We'll get this sorted out soon. Then you can go home."

"I don't really have a home to go to."

Cassie didn't know what to say, but Harris saved her by stepping in and placing a comforting hand on Rose's shoulder. "I know it's going to be hard, but relax as much as you can. We'll keep you updated. Right now, your only concern is your baby, okay?"

Rose nodded, peering up at Harris with a determined look on her face. "I've thought about what you said last night."

"About testifying?" Harris tried not to look hopeful, but Cassie could see right through her. She'd asked Rose if she'd be willing to go to court against Aguilar. The other woman had been visibly alarmed by the thought, and she hadn't given them a straight answer.

Rose nodded. "I'll do it. For Randall. I know he made mistakes. But he was brave enough to do the right thing in the end. I want to make sure it wasn't in vain."

"He'd be proud of you, Rose." Harris's voice was full of emotion. "I know it."

One of the men next to Rose cleared his throat, and the three of them turned to leave. Cassie watched through her tears as they got into a big black SUV and drove away. She and Harris climbed back into their little gold Toyota and waited until they could no longer see the other vehicle in the distance.

After a minute of silence, Cassie sighed, and Harris looked over at her from the driver's seat. "What's up?"

"Nothing." Cassie shifted around uncomfortably when Harris shot her another look. "It's just a lot." She threw her hands up and gestured wildly. They'd packed their bags and thrown them into the trunk in case they needed a quick getaway. It was finally hitting her. "All of this. And I'm not really looking forward to paying Reed another visit."

"Reed's a slimeball, but he knows something." Harris tapped the Annex folder sitting on the console between them. "We just gotta get him to slip up and tell us something we don't already know."

"Good luck with that," Cassie grumbled. "He wasn't exactly impressed the last time we were there."

"We played nice the last time we were there."

Cassie didn't know what not playing nice looked like, but she was too nervous to do anything but let Harris take the lead. This time, they parked a few blocks away from the office. With everyone closing in on them from all angles, Harris thought it was smart to keep their distance. Cassie wasn't so sure. What if they needed a quick getaway?

Nothing had changed about the office from the last time they'd visited, from the ratty rug at the entrance to the worn banister that led upstairs to their target. Even the putrid stench of the janitor's water clung to the air, and Cassie was not surprised to see him standing down the hall, one hand on his mop and both eyes trained on them.

Only there was a noticeable difference about him this time.

The long hair and beady eyes were the same, but his knuckles were swollen and scabbed over. Cassie had thought he'd already looked terrifying enough, but his wounds made a shiver travel down her spine. How had he gotten them?

If Harris was worried about it, she didn't let it show. Like last time, the detective glanced at the man and then promptly ignored him, taking the stairs two at a time until she was on the second floor. By the time Cassie caught up, Harris was already at the end of the hall with one hand on the doorknob into Don A. Reed's office.

She didn't bother knocking.

As Harris stormed into the office, Cassie came up behind her with a little more self-preservation. Reed was alone, and his office looked the same as last time, with files stacked across every surface, including the floor.

Reed's eyes narrowed when he realized who had just barged in. "Get out."

Harris didn't back down. "Not until you answer some questions."

"You took something that wasn't yours." He shook his head. "Big mistake."

"I don't know what you're talking about."

"I'm not afraid to get my hands dirty, lady." He held them up like they'd be able to spot the blood on them. "Don't stick your nose where it don't belong."

"Is that a threat?"

Reed stood, and another pile shifted and fell over. He ignored it. "I'm callin' the cops if you're not outta here in five seconds."

Harris reached into her pocket and grabbed her fake badge, slamming it down on the man's desk but leaving her hand to cover the front so he'd have no idea it wasn't real. "We're already here. And I have some questions you need to answer."

If Reed was nervous, he didn't show it. He sat down and waved her away. "I'm not answering shit."

"What's the purpose of Annex, LLC?" Harris didn't wait for him to answer. "Who's the owner? Is it Francis Aguilar?"

Reed looked up sharply. His lips were pursed. He didn't look afraid. More cautious than anything.

"Interesting." Harris grinned. She knew she was onto something. "You're a pretty shitty lawyer, you know. Surprised you still have your license. How'd you work that one out, considering how many times you've been arrested?"

"Never charged." He grinned back at her. "Never convicted."

"Doesn't mean you didn't do shit."

"Doesn't mean I did."

Harris slipped the badge back into her pocket, and Cassie

breathed a little easier. The last thing they needed was to be caught with that thing. Was it still impersonating an officer when you *were* a suspended officer? Cassie had a feeling she'd get in even more trouble than Harris. Was aiding and abetting just for fugitives?

"You deal with a lot of insurance fraud, don't you?" Harris inspected her fingernails. She was so calm and relaxed. Cassie was still shaking in the doorway. "In Savannah, too. Pretty interesting."

"What can I say. I get around."

Cassie felt the temperature rise again. Just a degree or two, but she felt it against her skin. On the back of her neck. Somewhere in the pit of her stomach. They were onto something with the insurance fraud. But how did it tie into everything else?

She decided to take a risk. One she hoped Harris would approve of. "What about the person you killed?" She took a step forward, and even Harris turned around to gape at her. The heat of the room pulsed, making her head swim. "Huh? Insurance fraud is one thing. Maybe you can cover that up with clever paperwork and a few friends down at the station, but what about murder? Where there's smoke, there's fire, right? And probably more than one body."

Reed froze, looking Cassie up and down like he was seeing her for the first time. Instead of answering, he swiped at a few folders and sent them to the floor, uncovering the desk phone. Picking it up, he held it to his ear, never breaking eye contact with Cassie. She started to sweat. And not just from the heat of the room.

"Get up here," he said into the receiver. "Now."

Less than fifteen seconds passed before they heard the creak of the floorboards in the hallway. When Cassie turned, she saw the janitor standing at the door, his beady black eyes trained on her face. A small smile played around on his lips, sending a cold shiver down her spine, wiping away the effects of the heat she'd been feeling.

"Escort these ladies out," Reed said. "And make sure they don't come back."

"No need." Harris's voice dripped with false cheer. "We know the way. It was nice seeing you again, Donny. Chat soon."

Harris placed a hand on Cassie's back, steering her out of the room and past the janitor. Neither wasted time descending the stairs and exiting the building. But Harris didn't turn in the direction of the car. Swinging left, she strolled down the sidewalk. When there was enough distance between them and the building. She turned to Cassie.

"What the hell was that?"

"What?" Cassie replied.

"Back there. Dead bodies? We didn't talk about that."

"Well, we didn't exactly go in with a plan, either," Cassie grumbled. Was Harris seriously pissed at her? "It just came to me."

"Came to you?"

"Yeah, came to me." Cassie rolled her eyes. "Honestly, you should be used to this by now."

"I'm never going to be used to you." Harris' shoulders relaxed a little. "You think that's what the shadow person is? A victim from one of those fires?"

"Every time we go into Reed's office, it gets hot. He's tied to it. But I still don't know how."

Harris nodded. "Then we have some more work to do."

32

DETECTIVE HARRIS WALKED FURTHER FROM THE BUILDING. CASSIE hesitated for only a second or two before she jogged to catch up. She hooked a thumb over her shoulder. "But the car is back that way."

Harris spoke with the patience of a parent explaining something simple to their child. "We don't want them to know where we parked."

"You think they'll follow us?"

"I guarantee it."

Cassie bit back a groan of panic and looked over her shoulder. Sure enough, the janitor had emerged from the building and leaned against the wall. He rolled his sleeves up to his elbows, then took a cigarette from his pocket and lit it. He didn't look in their direction, but Cassie had a feeling he was still watching them.

She turned back around. "I don't have a good feeling about this."

"Is that a regular feeling or a special feeling?"

Cassie bit back a laugh. "A regular feeling. I think."

"Regular feelings I can deal with." Harris swerved to the right at a crosswalk and jogged across it, just as the timer ran out. "Come on. Keep up."

Cassie didn't need to be told twice. She resisted the urge to look over her shoulder again. Harris clearly had a plan, and Cassie didn't want to mess it up. But she had a constant tingle against the back of her neck. Turning around would scratch the itch, but it'd make the threat much more real.

Harris took a left when they got to the other side of the street and then turned right, putting even more distance between them and the car. Cassie knew she was doing it for a reason. But it felt like they were cutting themselves off from their only means of escape.

Lost in thought, Cassie almost crashed into Harris when she stopped in front of a building, contemplating whether it was their salvation. After a moment, she gestured Cassie after her. "Come on. Let's go inside."

Cassie looked at the marquee above her head. It was for a Mediterranean restaurant called Zesty. The outside looked normal. Like most of the other buildings on the block, it showed its age but had a certain classic charm.

As soon as Harris opened the door, Cassie could smell the herbs in the air. Despite having had breakfast only an hour or two ago, it made her mouth water.

"We're getting lunch?" Cassie whispered. "Now? Really?"

Harris ignored her. A woman wearing a waist apron walked up to them with a huge smile on her face. Her skin was a beautiful golden brown, and she had thick eyebrows above mesmerizing hazel eyes. Cassie had to blink a few times to make sure she was real. That was someone who should've been on movie screens, not stuck working in a restaurant for measly tips.

"Two today?" the woman asked.

"Three, actually. We're meeting a friend." Harris leaned around the woman and pointed somewhere on the other side of the dining room. It was packed, and even from where Cassie stood, she couldn't figure out who the detective was pointing at. "There she is. Mind if we seat ourselves?"

"Not at all." The waitress stepped to the side. "Go right ahead."

"Thank you." Harris gave the other woman a wink.

When the two of them were out of earshot, Cassie tapped the

detective on the shoulder. "Are you sure it's a good idea to lie low in here?" she asked. "What if he waits for us outside?"

Harris still had a giant grin on her face. "Trust the process."

Cassie didn't know what that meant, but she'd spent enough time with Harris to know when the woman had an ace up her sleeve. And sure enough, by the time they crossed the busy dining room— dodging servers and making sure to not knock over anyone's drinks— Harris had changed directions, pointing them toward the kitchen's swinging doors.

With no hesitation, the detective pushed through the doors, and Cassie stumbled in after her. While the dining room had been dark and cozy, the kitchen was a riot of bright light and noise. Not only were there men and women shouting at each other in a variety of languages, but the sizzling pans and buzzing of timers made the entire place impossible to digest. Cassie felt her gaze bouncing between one station and the next.

"Hey!" someone shouted. "You can't be in here."

Harris held up her hands. "Sorry, sorry. Just trying to get out the back."

The man stepped up to them. He wore a chef's uniform and hat. His apron was messy, but his hands were clean. And one of them was holding a butcher's knife. "You can't be in here. Go back out."

"Please," Harris begged. There was a raw emotion to her voice that Cassie had never heard before. "A guy's been following us for, like, three blocks. We're really scared."

The man looked between the two women. Cassie had to guess he was in his fifties. Maybe he had a couple of daughters. He grunted. "What kind of man?" he asked.

"We don't know him," Harris said. She wrung her hands, and the man didn't miss the movement. "He just kept saying stuff to us. Rude stuff. It scared us. We were hoping to go out the back. Is there an alley back there?"

The man nodded. "Yeah, leads to the next street."

Harris's eyes lit up, and Cassie felt hope blossom in her chest. "That's all we need," the detective said. "Please, we won't cause any trouble. We just want to get to the next street over so we can circle back to our car. We didn't want him seeing where we parked and getting our license plate."

The funny part was, most of that wasn't a lie.

The chef nodded his head and gestured for them to follow him. A few of the cooks gave them a passing glance, but they mostly tried to keep up with their orders. From the looks of it, the food was as good as it smelled.

When they reached the back door, the man pushed it open for them and checked both ways. It must've been clear because he moved to the side and let them back outside. "Go that way," he said, pointing to the right. "Then cross the street again and go another block. Then circle back to your car. Safer that way."

"Thank you, sir," Harris said, stepping outside.

Cassie squeezed by the man, careful to avoid the blade still in his hand. "Yes, thank you. We really appreciate it."

"Stay safe," he said, giving them a fatherly look.

Harris raised her hand in thanks and walked toward the end of the alley, Cassie on her heels. When they made it to the sidewalk, they both turned back around and gave the chef another wave. He nodded his head and ducked back inside.

No sooner had he disappeared than Cassie heard a grunt and Harris was knocked to the ground, landing on the asphalt on her hands and knees. Two big hands grabbed ahold of Cassie, one wrapping around her mouth and the other bringing one of her arms behind her back. Pain shot through her shoulder, and she cried out.

Cassie didn't need to turn around to know who it was. She could smell the putrid water wafting off him. His tattooed hands were dirty, and she could taste bleach on her lips. Maybe he was a janitor after all.

Or maybe he used bleach for other purposes.

Cassie refused to let him get the upper hand. As Harris got back to her feet, Cassie drew her head forward and drove it back as hard as she could. She felt a satisfying crunch as the man's nose broke and he cried out in pain. She took the opportunity to pull out of his loosened grip.

Turning around to face him, she put several feet between them. The man drew his hand away from his face and took in the blood that had pooled into his palm. Then he looked up at Cassie with a snarl. "You bitch. You're gonna—"

Harris didn't let him get another word out. She charged at him, kicking his knee, and sending him to the ground. He was back on his feet a second later, swinging at her. She blocked his punches with one arm and delivered a jab to his already broken nose. He howled in pain.

Onlookers scurried by the alley, curious about what was going on but not wanting to get involved. Cassie wondered if that was why Harris hadn't drawn her gun—too many witnesses and too many opportunities for someone else to get hurt. A fistfight would get them into less trouble than armed assault.

Harris kept up the barrage of blows, alternating between his face and his stomach. He blocked most of them. A few landed against his gut. He looked unaffected, despite the few grunts he let out.

Cassie noticed too late that he was trying to wear Harris down. She was putting all her energy into her blows, favoring her injured shoulder, and he was absorbing them. Harris must've figured it out too because she switched to using her feet, aiming for his kneecaps and groin.

The man was fast for his size. As Harris went to land another blow, he stepped into the attack and grabbed her leg, pinning it to his side. Then he feigned a shot to her bad shoulder, and when she tried to dodge, he used her own momentum against her. He slammed her to the ground and landed a punch in her gut. Cassie practically felt it in her own body.

As he reared back for another punch, Cassie charged at him, taking him by surprise. She wasn't sure what she planned to do aside from distract him, but she'd fight tooth and nail to get him off Harris. It had to be enough.

And it was. As his hand shot out to stop her, Harris kicked him between the legs with the heel of her boot. The man curled in on himself, and Cassie sidestepped his arm, lowered her center of gravity, and drove her shoulder into his side.

Not expecting the sheer force of the momentum she'd built up in her run, the man tripped over Harris's legs and went tumbling out of the alleyway and onto the sidewalk. The crowd that had formed near the entrance shrieked in unison and started to back up, pulling out their phones.

The janitor recovered faster than Harris or Cassie. "Help!" he yelled. He pointed a finger at the two women. "Help! I'm being attacked! She has a gun!"

The crowd gasped and turned their collective attention toward Harris, who scurried to her feet and tugged her coat tighter around her waist, hiding her firearm from their prying eyes. She turned to Cassie as she backpedaled. Only one word came out of her mouth.

"Run."

33

Zbirak picked up his phone with a scowl. He was at home, meditating, having left poor Robert Sherman to worry about his family. Don Reed knew that, yet he called anyway. Burrowing into his brain like a parasite. Zbirak hated working with the man, but Reed had connections. And Aguilar liked him. For some goddamn reason.

Then there was that little piece of history they shared together. A job gone wrong. He had bailed Reed out of a tight situation on the West Coast. Reed had his hands in many pots, and Zbirak had been smart enough to take advantage of an opportunity when it arose. But now they were connected, and he was beginning to doubt it had been worth the trouble. The man gave lawyers a bad name.

Zbirak lifted the phone to his ear. He didn't bother with pleasantries. "What?"

"Why are the cops knocking down my door?" Reed's voice was flush with anger. "Who sent them here? Huh? Was it you?"

"You'll watch your tone when you speak to me." Zbirak didn't need to present any more of a threat than that. His reputation preceded him. "We both know that if I had an issue with you, I wouldn't send you to jail. I'd make you dig your own grave."

Reed's tone was still gruff, but it had lost some of its bite. "Two bitches showed up at my office. Twice. One of them had a badge."

Zbirak bit back his retort about Reed's language. It was a lost cause. And Zbirak was more interested in getting to the bottom of this interruption. "Why didn't you call me the first time?"

"I'm not one of your groupies," Reed spat. "I can handle my own shit."

"Clearly not." Zbirak let his words hang between them, waiting to see if Reed was stupid enough to take the bait. When the silence stretched on, Zbirak continued. "Why were they there?"

"They had questions. About Annex. Stole one of my folders the other day. Then had the balls to come back and rub it in my face."

Zbirak already had perfect posture, otherwise he would've sat up ramrod straight. "What was in the folder?"

"Just some shit about Annex. Insurance claims. All legit, more or less."

Zbirak very much doubted that. "Anything that can be traced back to our friend?"

Reed scoffed. "You mean Aguilar? No."

"You know the rules."

"Whatever, man. Look, I have some shit going down, okay? I can't have them poking around here. You gotta get rid of them."

"I'll remind you, *Donald*, that I do not work for you. And you have no authority to give me such demands."

Reed groaned. "I know you get off being in control and all that bullshit, but you gotta do something, man."

"Send your little lap dog after them."

"I already did," Reed ground out, and Zbirak could imagine the fire in the other man's eyes. "That dark-haired bitch beat the shit out of him."

Zbirak tried to keep the anger from his voice, but it was nearly impossible. "What happened?"

"Tried to jump them in an alleyway. They got away. Doesn't know where they went."

"So, you lost them?"

"I didn't lose them, Tommy—"

"A good leader always takes responsibility for his subordinates."

"That's the difference between you and me, pal. I never said I was a good leader."

"You have descriptions? License plate? Anything."

"Security footage. Hang on." There was a shuffling of papers and some clicks of a button. "There. You get that?"

Zbirak heard a soft chime in his ear and lowered the phone, opening the text message from Reed. It contained a single photo, which was grainy and in black and white. But it was clear enough to make out two women. And one was easy enough to recognize.

"The dark-haired one is Detective Adelaide Harris. She was close with David Klein," Zbirak said.

"Who?" Reed asked.

"Never mind. Who was the other woman?"

"Hell if I know. Some red-headed bitch."

Zbirak pulled the phone away again to look at the image. The angle of the camera indicated it was up high, perhaps in the corner of the room. The other woman's head was tilted down and to the side, which made it almost impossible to identify her. He couldn't see her stomach, but her coat would've hidden her pregnant belly anyway. Still, who else would be poking their nose into their business?

Zbirak brought the phone back to his ear. "That's Rose Sherman, Randall's wife."

"Randy's wife?" Reed grunted. "What's she doing here? If she were smart, she'd be out of the country by now."

"Indeed." The gears in Zbirak's head started turning. "Tell Mr. Thompson that if he wants to redeem himself, to meet me back in our little fun room. He's got one hour."

Zbirak didn't bother waiting for an answer. If Thompson didn't show up, well, then his fate was sealed. Zbirak didn't tolerate failure, and he certainly didn't tolerate disobedience on top of that. Thompson might not have been much more than a petty criminal, but he'd prove his worth one way or another.

Now, Zbirak simply had to wait until curiosity got the better of the detective and her new friend. He knew enough about Adelaide Harris to know she wouldn't stop until she found answers. Patience was a virtue, and Zbirak had it in spades. This was his favorite part. He'd let his prey come to him. Then the fun would really begin.

34

CASSIE AND HARRIS WALKED HALF A MILE IN THE OPPOSITE DIRECTION, careful to check whether they were being followed. When the detective was satisfied, they wound their way back to where they started, taking their time, and doubling back often.

Harris made it to the car first. As soon as Cassie slid inside and slammed the door shut, the detective peeled away from the curb. Cassie couldn't help but look over her shoulders, trying to spot the man who'd attacked them only moments before. If he was still there, he blended into the crowd.

Cassie turned back around and buckled her seatbelt. She cast a glance at Harris, who spent every three seconds looking in her rearview mirror. The detective's face was passive, but her knuckles had turned white around the steering wheel.

"I didn't see him," Cassie said. "Did you?"

"No. Or Reed. Hopefully they didn't figure out where we parked."

"Why would he do that?" Cassie ran a hand down the side of her face. "Call for help, I mean. Wasn't he afraid of getting caught?"

"We were kicking his ass," Harris said. There was a slight chuckle in her voice. "Someone would've stopped it eventually, and it would've made him look bad. He was a lot worse for wear, so better for him to play the victim card."

"We should've stuck around and interrogated him."

"With my fake badge?" The detective shook her head. "Wouldn't have worked. Besides, I don't know about you, but I don't want my face in a viral video."

"Me neither." Cassie sighed. Had they even accomplished anything? "And now we lost him."

"Did you notice his tattoo?"

"I wasn't taking notes."

Harris smirked. She had stopped checking the rearview mirror. Her knuckles loosened on the wheel, and she used one hand to rub her injured shoulder. They were out of danger. For now. "It was a mermaid tattoo."

"And that's important because?" Cassie's eyes got wide as the detective let her figure it out for herself. "The guy that hired Armando and his friend to clean out the jewelry shop. That was him."

"Yep."

"So, wait a second." Cassie's head was filled with so many connections, she couldn't see straight. "Randall Sherman's flash drive led us to the jewelry store, which the janitor hired those guys to clean out. The janitor works for Reed, who has a record of shady insurance claims, including those found in Savannah."

"Everything is coming full circle." Harris's grin was dark. "We just need one more link."

"Putting Aguilar in the middle."

"Basically."

Cassie tipped her head back and stared at the ceiling of the Corolla. "But how? Reed is onto us. The janitor has already proven he's willing to attack us in broad daylight. We're lucky Rose is gone. She's their prime target. They think she knows something."

"And whoever was on the phone still has Bob. We need to figure out where they are."

"Or draw them out somehow." Cassie sat up straight, inspiration flashing before her eyes. "Oh."

"Oh?" Harris looked over at her, eyes sharp. "What do you mean, *oh*?"

"It's a little darker than hers, but it could work. Maybe she dyed it."

"Cassie, what the hell are you talking about."

Cassie grinned, and she knew it looked wicked. "I have red hair."

"Yeah. I see that." Harris shook her head. "So what?"

"Rose has red hair."

"Okay?"

"They don't know we sent Rose away. And as soon as we turn on that phone—"

"No way." Harris sat up straight in her seat, shaking her head back and forth vigorously. "No freaking way."

"Hear me out." Cassie waited until Harris sat still. "As soon as we turn on the phone, that guy will know where we are. We tell him Rose is volunteering to trade herself for Bob. She'll tell him whatever he wants to know as long as she gets to walk out of there in the end. She'll disappear. She won't tell anyone anything."

"There's no guarantee he'll agree to that. And even if he does, we won't know if he'll keep his word."

Cassie ignored her and continued. "We trade Bob for Rose. Obviously, I'll be Rose." Harris started shaking her head again, but Cassie pushed on. "Once Bob is clear, and this guy thinks he can relax, you'll storm in and take him out."

"Take him out?" Harris rolled her eyes. "Are you even listening to yourself right now?"

"It's gonna work."

"There are so many ways this could go wrong. We can't risk it."

Cassie was barely listening. "Let's assume he'll have some sort of trick up his sleeve. I'll need a GPS tracker. That way, you'll be able to follow him."

"What if he takes you to a compound? What if he's not alone? What if he kills you as soon as he grabs you? It's too risky."

"He's not going to kill me right away. He'll want to know if I told you anything. You'll know he took me, so he'll need to wait for you to arrive anyway. He won't be happy with you as a loose end. I'll just need to hold out long enough for you to arrive."

"*Hold out long enough*? Cassie, listen to yourself. He'll torture you."

"I've been through worse." Her voice came out quiet. Small. "I can handle it."

Harris was silent for what felt like an eternity. "And if he's not alone? I can't take out a whole team of guys by myself."

"Then go to the cops, show them the GPS, and say I've been kidnapped. If this guy works for Aguilar, he won't spend any time in jail for kidnapping. Might be a different story for murder. He won't risk it. Trust me."

"Trust you? This is suicide."

"It's going to work." Cassie infused her voice with as much confidence as she could muster. "I know it is. I have a feeling."

"A feeling?"

"Yeah."

"A special feeling?"

Cassie's stomach twisted away from the lie, but she pushed through the nausea. "Yes. A special feeling."

Harris sighed. It wasn't an ideal situation, but what other choice did they have?

"Fine. But you have to do what I say. No going off on your own. You understand?" She looked over at Cassie with piercing eyes. "This is only going to work if we're smart about it. Don't play the hero. There's no point in saving Bob if you end up getting shot."

"I understand." The scope of what they were about to do finally hit Cassie, and her stomach roiled again. "Don't play the hero."

"Well, you know what we need to do next then, don't you?"

"What's that?"

A sad, weary smirk spread across the detective's face. "Figure out how to make you pregnant."

35

GUILT WRACKED HARRIS'S BODY. SHE'D BEEN TOO CAVALIER ABOUT THIS whole situation. Dogged determination was one of her strengths, and one of her weaknesses. Sometimes when she set her sights on a goal, she didn't care how she got there. And Cassie might end up paying the price.

Inhale. Exhale. Inhale. Exhale.

One breath at a time, she cleared her mind. It was difficult considering the amount of people surrounding her. The mall was packed for the holiday season, and they were smack dab in the middle of the cafeteria. Hundreds of people passed through every hour. But it was the easiest way to keep Cassie safe. Too many witnesses for anything big to go down.

Harris refocused, going over the plan in her mind again. The best way to make Cassie look pregnant was to strap a hotel pillow to her stomach. Not exactly high-tech, but after securing it in place and putting on a large sweater, the effect looked real. She'd told Cassie to keep placing her hands on her stomach, and even wincing in discomfort every once in a while. It was a worthy performance. They'd even had a few women come up to her and ask if she needed anything.

One lady had reached out a hand to touch Cassie's stomach, but

Cassie swatted it away. Harris had to bury her face in her arm to keep from laughing too loudly.

But seriously. The gall of some people.

While Cassie had gotten dressed, Harris had run out to the store. She picked up a GPS tracking device, and they'd stuffed it into the center of the pillow. She'd also bought a set of comms, so they'd never be out of communication. Technology was truly amazing. The earbuds were beige in color and tiny, meaning they could both hide them with their hair. Even if the comms were discovered, they had the GPS as a backup.

Not that any of this made Harris feel better.

"I've got a bad feeling about this," Harris muttered.

There was a crackle of static, and Cassie's quiet voice came through loud and clear. "Well, I don't. It's going to work."

Harris appreciated Cassie's confidence, even if she didn't share it. There was something about the way Cassie had said she had a *special feeling* that didn't sit right with Harris. Harris trusted Cassie, but that didn't mean Cassie wouldn't lie to get to the bottom of this.

To learn what happened to David.

Harris shook the thought from her head. She had to stay focused on Cassie. Once they got Bob back and figured out who was after Rose, then she could think about David. Solve his murder. Drink herself into oblivion for causing it.

The detective scanned the crowd, using the distraction to push David out of her mind—for now. There were all sorts of people here today. Young and old, single and in pairs. Large families with screaming children and grumpy teenagers.

Cassie had sat herself at a table right in the middle of all the chaos. Harris had kept to the outskirts of the cafeteria with a direct line of sight on the other woman. Despite sitting at a table meant for four, no one bothered Cassie. One of the perks of looking pregnant, at least.

But people kept shooting Harris dirty looks for sitting at her table for two without any food in front of her. Real estate in the cafeteria was sparse, and it was everyone for themselves. She wasn't going to give up her spot so easily. She'd happily fight anyone here.

Harris scanned the crowd again, looking for any familiar faces. Someone she'd seen circling the court a few times already. Her gaze landed on a tall, lean man with brown hair. He was conventionally attractive, if not a little average. Plain. He shouldn't have stuck out in the crowd. But it was the third time she'd noticed him traversing the room, as though looking for someone. Only he didn't look like a person searching for a friend or a loved one.

The way his gaze landed on every single face—assessing them, cataloging them—he looked like a predator on the hunt.

Harris kept the movement of her lips to a minimum. "Text him."

Cassie didn't answer, but Harris saw her look down at her phone and type out a message. Harris's eyes snapped back to the man in the crowd. A few seconds later, he pulled out his phone and stared down at it. A smile crept over his face. His shoulders relaxed. He stood up a little taller.

The predator had found its prey.

"I've got eyes," Harris mumbled. She saw Cassie squirm in her seat in response. "Easy. Breathe. Remember the plan. I'm right here. Keep it cool. No matter what happens, I'm coming for you. Got it?"

Cassie's voice was low, almost a whisper, but it came through loud and clear for Harris. "Got it."

Harris peeled her gaze from Cassie and searched the crowd for their man. But he was no longer standing in the same spot. Her heart rate spiked, afraid she'd lost him, and she had to remind herself to stay calm. She knew where Cassie was, and that was the most important part. He'd come to them.

Harris twisted in her seat, as though nonchalantly searching for a friend. She was really checking behind her, making sure their guy hadn't spotted her and changed tactics. Although, he'd have even less luck with her. She might be on the periphery of the cafeteria, but she wouldn't go quietly.

Harris couldn't spot him anywhere. Her heart rate spiked again, especially when she felt a presence at her back. Goosebumps erupted along her arms underneath the sleeves of her jacket, telling her someone was standing next to her. Too close.

When she turned, the first thing she spotted was a forearm rippling with muscle. And a mermaid tattoo with what looked like dried blood splattered across her face.

The second thing she saw was a fist careening toward her.

But Harris had been on edge since they stepped foot into the mall, and she was ready for anything. When the janitor's fist neared her eye, she threw up an arm to block it. It glanced off and clipped the top of her head, but at least she'd saved her orbital bone from shattering.

It had unbalanced the man enough for her to slip from the chair and land a blow to the side of his kneecap.

Screams erupted around her. After all, it wasn't every day that a tattooed, greasy-haired tank of a man—who already had a broken nose—attacked a young woman in broad daylight. Amidst the chaos, Harris couldn't help wondering what the play was. There was no way this guy was gonna get away with throwing punches. Someone was likely to jump in and help her.

Right?

Never one to let someone else finish a fight she didn't start, Harris crossed her arms in front of her face and blocked the man's kick. It sent her sliding back a few inches, and that was enough room to get to her feet. She squared off with the guy, a wicked grin on her face.

"This didn't work out so well for you last time," Harris said.

"There were two of you last time," the man growled. "Wasn't a fair fight."

"And getting the drop on me was?"

He shrugged. "Your fault for not paying better attention."

Harris didn't bother responding. She had to lay this guy out quick and get to Cassie. With the other man still in the crowd, there was no telling what would happen. And with all the screaming and yelling, she couldn't hear Cassie in her ear.

So, it was time to go on the offensive. Harris kicked out with her right leg, careful not to let him catch it like he had last time. The blow missed him by inches, but she was already swinging with her right arm. Her fist connected with his cheekbone, but it was like punching a slab of meat. He didn't even stumble.

In retaliation, the man threw a series of quick jabs, which Harris absorbed with tightened stomach muscles. It hurt, but it didn't knock out her breath, and she stood tall. Sucking in stale air, she stepped closer, feigning a jab to his gut with her right arm and coming in with a left hook that connected with his temple.

It was hard and fast enough to knock the sense out of him for a second or two, and that was all the time she needed. Harris kicked out with her leg again, and when she connected with his kneecap a second time, she felt a satisfying crunch, indicating she'd dislocated it from the socket. The man howled in pain and dropped to his good knee.

It was the perfect height to allow her to bring her own knee up into his face. And with that, she heard the satisfying crunch of his nose for the second time that day. But she didn't stop there. With his head tilted back, she spun and landed a kick to the side of his head.

And he dropped to the floor like a bag of bricks.

"Holy shit."

Harris looked up to find a tall, muscular man looking between her and the janitor. It was obvious he'd been trying to find an opening to step in between the two of them, but the fight had been over so quickly, he hadn't had a chance.

"I'm a cop," Harris said. She didn't bother pulling out her badge. "Keep an eye on him. Don't let him get up. Shout if he moves."

The other man nodded dumbly and looked back down at the unconscious janitor.

Harris sprinted through the crowd, calling Cassie's name. Something was wrong with the comms. She thought the crowd had been too loud, but now she realized there was dead silence on the other end.

When Harris skidded to a stop in front of Cassie's table, her heart sank into her stomach. A wave of nausea hit her so hard, she stumbled and fell to her knees. It took several breaths to clear her head enough to comprehend what she was looking at.

An open phone on the table. An earpiece on the floor, smashed to bits. A chair tipped over, like its former occupant had been dragged out of it. Harris had to swallow back bile as she realized what had happened. The janitor was merely the distraction.

Cassie was gone.

36

CASSIE COULD HARDLY SEE WHERE SHE WAS GOING. THE CROWD SURGED around her, bodies jostling her this way and that. She kept her face down to protect it from flying elbows. The only constant was the tight grip around her bicep and the sharp point pressing into her side.

She had gotten a single glimpse of Harris as the janitor attacked before the entire cafeteria erupted into chaos. Everyone started screaming and running in different direction. A teenager had run clean into her, spilling her from the chair and knocking the comms device out of her ear. She heard the crunch of it underfoot as the kid ran in the other direction with a hasty apology.

Strong arms lifted her from the ground and dragged her away from the table. At first, she let him take her away, scared she'd be trampled underfoot. But as the distance increased between her and Harris, Cassie pulled away, telling the man she needed to get back to her friend.

That's when he'd shoved the tip of an icepick into her side and told her to keep moving.

Unsure of what else to do, she obeyed. Harris would be fine handling the janitor, especially if someone from the crowd stepped in to help. Cassie had to worry about herself now. The icepick dug into her side every time someone bumped into the man, and she winced in pain. It felt like it was drawing blood already, and things would get much worse if he decided to teach her a lesson.

Cassie took a chance and looked up from his polished shoes to peer into his face. He was a good-looking man with dark hair and bright, roving eyes. When he looked down to meet her gaze, he smiled, and for a second, she was dazzled.

But then the icepick dug a little deeper, and she let out a gasp.

"I'll scream," she said, her voice barely audible over the crowd.

"You'll do no such thing, Mrs. Sherman." The man was poised and polite. "Or I'll let you stay alive long enough to feel your baby die inside of you."

Cassie ground her teeth together. On the plus side, the man thought she was Rose. On the downside, once he figured out she wasn't, Cassie would pay the price. The pillow might be able to protect her against an initial attack if he was aiming for the baby, but it would only take him seconds to realize his mistake.

Then he'd be able to drive the weapon into her side. Her chest. Her brain.

"You wouldn't hurt a baby, would you?" The sob that escaped her voice was real. "You're a monster."

"I've been called much worse, Mrs. Sherman." Licking his lips, there was a hunger in his eyes as he dragged her toward the exit. "And yes, I would kill an unborn child if it came between me and what I want. Although, I'll admit I would rather avoid that scenario."

Cassie didn't know what to say. If she screamed and managed to escape, they would lose their chance to find Bob. "Detective Harris will find you. She won't let you get away with this."

"Doubtful, even if Thompson manages to let her escape twice in one day."

Thompson must've been the janitor's name, further confirming the man chasing Rose and the lawyer were working together. But she still couldn't see the big picture. She needed more time. They were too close to the exit now. And as soon as they hit the outside air, there was no telling what he would do or where he would take her.

As the crowd funneled through the doors and onto the sidewalk outside, Cassie dug her heels in, but was rewarded with a sharp pinch to her side. The icepick had broken skin, and she gasped in response.

The man leaned down to whisper in her ear. "Mrs. Sherman, I suggest you don't struggle. This pick is long enough to spear your baby through the head. Not to mention your own vital organs. Death will be slow and painful. Trust me when I say you do not want that."

"What are you going to do with me?" she croaked.

"Ask you some questions. That's all."

She very much doubted that. "And Bob? You'll let him go?"

"Yes, I will let him go. If you're quiet and do as you're told."

Cassie bit back a retort. The plan might not have gone how they'd wanted it to, but was it different than they'd expected? Harris didn't have Bob yet, but they'd come up with an alternative if Cassie was kidnapped. The GPS tracking beacon was buried deep inside the pillow, where the man would never find it. As soon as Harris had Thompson under control, she'd come after Cassie. Nothing would happen to her. She could survive long enough to be rescued.

That thought alone was enough for Cassie to straighten her back as the man pulled her through the doors. A small gasp escaped her mouth when the winter air hit her in the face. Before she knew it, she was away from the rest of the crowd and around the side of the building. The man pulled her across the parking lot, never letting up the pressure on her side, until they stood in front of a black panel van with tinted windows.

"Your chariot awaits," the man said, chuckling to himself. "Are you going to give me any problems?"

"No, sir." What other answer was there?

"Good. I like you, Rose. You're a smart woman."

Cassie just gulped. "I-I don't even know your name."

"I have many names. I'm awfully fond of Zephyr. Do you like Greek mythology, Rose?"

"Y-yes." Cassie did, actually. "Zephyrus was the Greek god of the western wind."

"Very good. He was also the gentlest of the winds. Isn't that funny?"

She didn't think so, but something told her this man would punish dishonesty, so she kept her mouth shut. He seemed to understand her dilemma and smiled, releasing the icepick from her side and placing it in his pocket. But the grip around her bicep never loosened, not even when he leaned over and opened the side door of the van.

"My real name is Joseph Zbirak." He looked lost in thought for a moment. "I think I would like you to call me Mr. Zbirak."

"Okay." It was all she could squeak out. It felt like there was no air in her lungs.

"Would you like me to call you Rose or Mrs. Sherman?"

"R-Rose."

He nodded politely. "In you go, Rose."

Zbirak didn't give Cassie a chance to protest. He simply lifted her into the van and sat her on the bench seat, where he handcuffed each arm to a steel loop protruding from the side of the vehicle. Then he buckled her into place, careful not to jostle her pregnant belly.

He peered down at her, assessing her situation. "I suppose that's not very comfortable, but you're in for a bit of a ride, Rose. We'll be there soon enough."

As Zbirak shut the door, Cassie felt a tear slide down her cheek. Trusting Harris to do everything she could to find her, Cassie still couldn't help the doubt that crept in. The farther she got away from Harris, the harder it would be for the detective to find her. Two words sprang to mind, and she wished she could send them directly into Harris's brain.

Please hurry.

37

Joseph Zbirak was nothing like Cassie imagined. On the phone, he had been calm and collected, though not cold. He'd been in good humor, which had struck her as odd. That was nothing compared to how he was in real life. It was a strange way to describe someone so calculating and dangerous, but it was the only word she could think of to describe him.

Polite.

Of course, that was cancelled out by the fact she was handcuffed in the back of a panel van, headed to who knew where.

Cassie struggled against her bonds, but there was no hope. They were cinched tight enough around her wrists that she wouldn't be able to slip out. And the metal anchors bolted to the side of the van definitely weren't going anywhere.

All she could do was wait and see what happened next.

They drove for over an hour. Maybe longer. She could feel the difference between Lake Shore Drive and the countryside. The roads were rougher, and there wasn't as much traffic. The stopping and starting made her nauseous, seated the way she was in the back.

For his part, Zbirak stayed quiet. He'd put on some light jazz and drummed his fingers along the steering wheel. Sometimes he'd hum along to a song she didn't recognize. If they'd been in different circumstances, he'd look like nothing more than a delivery driver, happy to be going about his day.

It didn't take long for Cassie to figure out he was much more than that. The van smelled of bleach and orange. The back was like a mobile workstation, with a couple of shelves bolted to the side opposite her. There were drawers full of mysterious objects that rattled around every time they turned a corner. There were also tools hanging off hooks in the back. Hammers and saws and electric trimmers.

Everything was spotlessly clean. If anyone saw the inside of the van, they'd think Zbirak was a maintenance man or a lawn care service worker. But she had a feeling these tools weren't just for show. They were practical. Which meant he likely used them on human beings. And he was a lot more dangerous than he initially appeared to be.

For the first time, a trickle of fear slid down Cassie's back and into the pit of her stomach. She'd been in terrible situations before, it was true, but that never made it any easier. And now she had no choice but to wait for Harris to find her. They'd left her personal items at the hotel, so Zbirak wouldn't discover that she wasn't Rose Sherman. The comms device had been knocked out, and Rose's phone had been left behind. All she had to rely on was the GPS device, and a lot of luck.

Now, she regretted acting so confident all of this would work out.

It was too late to take it back. As the van rolled to another stop, Zbirak cut the engine and hopped out onto loose gravel. Cassie's heart rate kicked up a notch, and she could feel the sweat pooling in her palms. Taking a deep breath, she calmed her mind. All she had to do was outlast Zbirak and keep Bob alive.

How hard could that be?

The door to the van slid open, and Zbirak slipped inside, barely rocking the vehicle back and forth. He was a slight man, but up close, she could see how toned he was, even through his jacket. He didn't look big, but there was no doubt he could take care of himself. And he'd probably be fast, too.

"I hope the ride wasn't too uncomfortable for you, Rose."

Cassie debated how she should respond. She decided to reciprocate his civility. "Not ideal, but I'm doing okay."

"Wonderful." He smiled, looking like he meant it. "Now, I'm going to let you free. Are we going to have any problems?"

"No, sir."

He hummed, as though he appreciated her courtesy. "Good. Please remember that my previous threats still stand. I will kill your baby and let it die inside you. Then I will kill your husband's cousin and make you watch. I may even keep you alive long enough to kill the detective. Do you understand?"

"Yes, sir."

Zbirak nodded his head and produced a key to unlock the cuffs around her wrists. Then he hopped out of the van and held out his hand. Cassie took it, careful to make it look like she was struggling around her large stomach. He took much of her weight as she stepped down to the ground. They were in a driveway.

"Where are we?" she asked.

The house was small and dilapidated. Zbirak looked out of place standing in front of it. He was too clean and poised to live somewhere like this. It was likely just a place he kept to hold people hostage. And torture them. And probably kill them.

"One of my many properties," he answered. "Come along."

Cassie followed him. He didn't seem worried about her escaping. The house was surrounded by a forest, and they were a long way from anywhere populated. Even if she did manage to slip into the trees, a pregnant woman wouldn't be hard to catch.

Maybe Cassie could use that to her advantage. If she shed the pillow and hung onto the GPS unit, would she be able to outrun him? Outsmart him? Maybe, but she doubted it. He would know these woods better than her. Besides, all he had to do was threaten Bob's life, and she'd have to return.

She hadn't gone this far just to watch Bob die at the finish line.

"Inside, please."

Zbirak held the front door open for her, and she stepped through the entrance. The house was old but clean. There was that smell of bleach again, and she had to wonder how many people had entered this house on their own two feet and left in a body bag. If they even got a body bag. Maybe they left in pieces, shoved into a trash bag like garbage.

Cassie stood in the middle of the empty living room and watched as Zbirak locked the door behind them. "Where's Bob?" she asked.

"Downstairs."

"Is he still alive?"

"Yes, of course. I've kept my word."

"Not exactly." Her heart played a drumline when he looked at her with a questioning eye. "You said you'd let Bob go and take me instead. Now you have both of us. You tricked us."

"Ah, so I did. I apologize for that, Rose." He took her gently by the elbow and led her through the kitchen, over to a door that led to the basement. "My offer still stands, however. I just need to know what you've told your friends. And make sure you understand what will happen if you talk on matters that aren't yours to discuss."

"I promise, I won't—"

"Please don't make promises you can't keep. That is the quickest way to make me angry."

Cassie clamped her mouth shut, allowing Zbirak to lead her downstairs. She took the steps one at a time, as though making sure to be extra careful not to trip and fall. Her captor never rushed her, and even gave her a gentle pat on the hand when she reached the bottom before leading her through another door and into a second room.

This room was darker, and all the tiny windows along the exterior walls had been boarded over. A single light hung from the ceiling, which Zbirak clicked on, as though his muscle memory knew exactly where it was.

The sudden influx of light made Cassie squint and turn away from the bulb. Once she could see again, she turned back and took in the figure of Bob Sherman, slumped over in a chair, his hands bound behind his back.

She gasped. "Is he—?"

"No, no. He's alive."

Zbirak took the man's chin in his hand and lifted it, so Cassie could get a look at his face. It was beaten to a pulp. His eyes were swollen, his nose and lips were bleeding, and there were deep purple bruises along his cheek and jaw. She saw him swallow, but when he tried to speak, nothing much came out.

"Stay quiet, Mr. Sherman. I'll bring you water in a moment." Zbirak gestured to an empty chair beside Sherman. "Please, take a seat, Rose."

Cassie hesitated. This was it. The point of no return. If she allowed herself to be tied up, there was no running from that. She'd have to resign herself to waiting for Harris to track her down.

Then again, hadn't she already hit the point of no return? As soon as she'd gotten into the man's van, it had been over. Now, there was no choice but to comply and keep up the ruse.

Cassie nodded and sat down in the chair. Zbirak smiled like he was proud that she had seen reason. It sent shivers down her spine. This man might be polite and gentle, but that scared her even more than someone who raged with violence. Zbirak was a cold-blooded killer. He was whip smart and calculating.

It wouldn't be easy to escape.

Drawing a rope from the ground behind her, he looped it around her wrists, securing them to the chair. But unlike Bob's restraints, he tied each of her hands to the legs of the chair rather than together. She assumed it was to keep her and the baby more comfortable.

When Zbirak walked around to face her, he brought another rope and looped it across her chest, keeping it well above her belly. His arm brushed her stomach, and she gasped. Zbirak froze. What if he felt the difference? What if he knew it was just a pillow?

"Did that hurt?" he asked.

"Y-Yes. Just a little. I'm sorry. I'm very sensitive right now."

Staring down at her for a moment, he nodded. "I'll endeavor to be more careful."

And he was. He finished looping the rope around her and tying it to the back of the chair without getting close to her stomach a second time. Then, without another word, he walked back up the stairs, closing the door behind him.

Cassie tested her restraints. The knots were tight, but they weren't constricting any blood flow. She could even wiggle back and forth, which meant there was room to slip out if she could loosen the parts around her hands. She just needed Zbirak to stay away long enough for her to work on escaping. The likelihood of that was low, but it at least gave her a glimmer of hope while she waited.

Maybe it would be enough.

38

"Bob? Bob, can you hear me?"

Cassie didn't want to whisper too loudly, unsure how much her voice would carry throughout the empty, un-insulated house.

"Bob?"

"Yeah?" The man's voice was raspy and sounded like every letter caused him pain.

"Are you okay?" That was a stupid question. "Is anything broken?"

"Just my nose." Managing to raise his head, he looked at her. She thought he blinked a few times, but his eyes were so swollen, it was hard to tell. "You're not Rose."

"Shh." Cassie worked her hands back and forth, trying to loosen the knots that bound them. "My name is Cassie Quinn, a friend of Rose's."

"Where is she?"

"Far away from here, and safe." Not that she knew where *here* was. "But you have to pretend I'm Rose, okay? Zbirak doesn't know who I really am. And he won't be happy with either of us if he figures it out."

Bob nodded his head in understanding. Good enough.

"If I can get out of this and untie you, do you think you can run?"

"My wife," he said, finding the energy to struggle against his own ropes. "My son. Are they—?"

"They're safe." As far as she knew. "And they can't wait till you come back home."

Grunting, his body sagged in relief.

"But Bob, I need to know if—"

The door at the top of the stairs opened, and Zbirak descended with a glass of water in each hand. Setting one on the ground next to Cassie's chair, he walked over to Bob with the other, grabbed the man's hair, and tilted his head back, bringing the glass to Bob's lips and letting him drink.

Bob didn't struggle or resist, slurping at the water with greed. It seemed this wasn't the first time they had done this dance, and Cassie wondered how well Zbirak was taking care of the other man. Enough to keep him alive and coherent, but a weakness in Bob told Cassie he'd been beaten, starved, and kept in one place for the last twenty-four hours.

The room didn't smell like urine or feces, so Zbirak was probably taking the man upstairs whenever he needed to relieve himself. That could be the opening she needed to get the upper hand. Pregnant women had to pee a lot, right?

After Bob finished the glass of water, Zbirak moved over to Cassie. "Are you thirsty?" he asked.

She shook her head. She didn't want him any closer to her than he already was. "Please, can you let him go?" She looked over at Bob. "You have me now. He has a wife and son. Please let him go."

"Even if I let him go, he wouldn't make it far. We're a long way from anywhere populated." Zbirak looked down at her with a mixture of curiosity and something unreadable. "But I promise not to hurt him as long as you answer my questions honestly."

"Okay." Cassie shifted in her seat to cover up an attempt to loosen the ropes around her wrists. "What do you want to know?"

"Your husband, Randall, attempted to betray a mutual friend of ours. That was not wise."

"Friend is a loose term," Cassie said, unable to keep the bite out of her voice.

He smiled. "The detective you've been working with, Adelaide Harris, met with him the night he died."

"You mean the night he was murdered."

"Yes, of course." Zbirak voice was impassive, uninterested. "On the night Randall was murdered, he met with Detective Harris. I need to know if he gave her any information."

"What kind of information?"

Zbirak didn't answer her right away. He studied Cassie for a few seconds, then turned toward Bob, reared his arm back, and drove his fist into the other man's face. Bob's head jerked back with such force that he tipped over in his chair, landing with a thud and a groan.

Cassie didn't bother hiding the fact that she was struggling against her bonds now. "What are you doing? You said you wouldn't hurt him!"

"I said I wouldn't hurt him as long as you answered honestly."

"I did!"

"No, you're evading the question. Biding your time. No one is coming for you, Rose. I can promise you that." Zbirak walked over and lifted Bob from the floor, setting him upright. He inspected the chair for a few seconds, as though he were more concerned with its well-being than the man's. Then he turned back to Cassie. "Did Randall give Detective Harris any information that wasn't his to share?"

"I don't know." When Zbirak moved toward Bob again, Cassie yelled out. "Wait! Wait. I'm really not sure. She said it's an open investigation, and she can't share certain information. Not even with me."

"What information has Randall shared with you?"

Cassie had been rubbing her hands back and forth, hoping to loosen the knot, but now she froze. "Please, I'm not trying to avoid the question, but I need you to be more specific."

"I'll give you the benefit of the doubt." Zbirak appeared calm and poised, but Cassie wondered how long that would last. "Let's start at the beginning. How much do you know about your husband's line of work?"

"He was an accountant," Cassie said slowly. Was it just her imagination, or could she move her arms a little more freely now? "He kept books for Francisco Aguilar. That's where most of our money came from."

"Very good." He nodded for her to continue. "And what do you know about Mr. Aguilar?"

"He's a businessman." Cassie swallowed. "A terrific one."

"Accurate. And what sort of business does he conduct?"

"Restaurants. Real estate. Um, I'm not sure what else. Randall never got too specific."

"And when did your husband decide to betray his employer?"

"I-I'm not sure." Cassie rushed on, in case Zbirak thought that was a non-answer. "I think he'd been thinking about it for a while." She looked down at her belly. "But once I got pregnant, our priorities changed."

"As they are wont to do." Zbirak tapped a finger against his chin. "I'm convinced Bob here doesn't know anything about your husband's work."

"He doesn't. That's why you need to let—"

"You're in no position to negotiate." Zbirak took a step closer. "Who are the only people you've been in direct contact with?"

"Bob," Cassie listed out slowly. She tried to think if Rose had done anything else since coming to Chicago. "And Detective Harris. I didn't know who else I could trust."

"Very well. At least the list is short."

Cassie froze. The room darkened around her in response to his words, and she couldn't tell if it was her vision fading or something else. "B-but you said you'd let him go."

"I regret to inform you that I lied, Rose." Zbirak's brow furrowed like he really did regret being dishonest with her. "You see, I'm in the business of tidying up loose ends. Killing the detective was meant to be a warning. We thought it was enough of a warning for Randall. He was an invaluable asset. You should be proud."

"Killing t-the d-detective?" The tips of her fingers were numb. The room grew darker. A shadow moved out of the corner of her eye. She thought she heard whispers coming from somewhere above her. Didn't he hear them?

"Detective Klein. His usefulness had expired. I had warned Mr. Aguilar not to trust him, but he didn't listen. Then Detective Klein became a liability."

A chill ran its way down her spine. She looked into Zbirak's face and fought to keep her emotions in check. "You killed David?"

Zbirak stilled. Staring at her, he cocked his head to one side, then the other. Then his eyes went vacant. Any hospitality he'd been harboring for her immediately disappeared. But the controlled calculation remained. "You look a lot like her, you know."

Cassie focused on keeping her breath even. "Who?"

"Rose." He smiled, and it was wicked. "Darker hair, thinner face, but you have the same bone structure. I'd only seen her picture a few times. Enough to spot her in a crowd. You looked familiar, and so I simply accepted the ruse."

"Ruse?" Cassie licked her lips. Her brain couldn't comprehend what he was saying. "What do you mean?"

"Oh, congratulations." Zbirak took a step back, as though to take all of her in, and then brought his hands together. A smile stretched across his face as he clapped for several seconds. The sound echoed around the room. "Not many people can get one over on me. You did a marvelous job. Right up until the moment I mentioned David."

"I'm not sure what—"

Zbirak stepped forward and grabbed the hem of her sweater. He lifted it, exposing the tight tank top they had stuffed the pillow into. It had been enough to hold the shape, giving the illusion of being pregnant. Still not giving in to his anger, Zbirak ripped the pillow free and began searching it. When he came across the GPS tracker, he shook his head. "You stupid girl."

Cassie's heart hammered. Her palms were sweaty. Enough that she could feel them slipping through the ropes. She just needed a little longer to break free. She almost laughed at the lunacy of that thought—sure, she could break free. Then what? This man was an assassin. How could she possibly hope to get the upper hand?

"I can explain—" she started.

Zbirak slapped her across the face, forcing Cassie to eat the rest of her words. Then he dropped the GPS tracker on the ground and stomped on it. That's all it took for it to burst open. Had Harris copied down the address in time? How long had it been since Cassie had arrived at the house? Where was the detective now?

Zbirak pulled himself together. His little outburst still stung, but Cassie couldn't see any trace of the anger that had flashed across his face. The room dimmed around her again, though he didn't seem to notice. Was she losing it, or was something else trying to break through?

"What is your real name?" He held up a finger. "It is not a good idea to lie to me."

She gulped. Not sure what else to do, she told him the truth. Maybe it would be enough to keep him occupied for a few more minutes. "Cassie Quinn."

Zbirak's eyes lit up. "Cassie Quinn." Then, to her shock, he smiled again. "That explains why you looked so familiar. I've heard wonderful things about you."

Her jaw went slack. "You have?"

"Of course. I've seen your file."

"My file?"

"Yes. Your file." The smile never left his face. "Apex is quite interested in you, Cassie Quinn."

There was that name again. Apex Publicity. The same one she'd outwitted in North Carolina. The same one that had approached her about a job in New Orleans. "You work for them?"

"I have completed jobs for them in the past, yes. They pay me well, though their selections are not as interesting as I would hope. But you?" He leveled a finger at her. "They have some curious things to say about you."

She couldn't help herself. "Like what?"

"That you're a psychic. I'm not one to believe in that sort of thing, but I can't deny you've led quite the interesting life." He leaned in closer. "Tell me, is it true? Can you really speak to the dead?"

Cassie slipped her thumb out of one of the loops around her wrist. She just needed a few more minutes to get free. "Let him go," she said, nodding toward Bob, "and I'll tell you everything you want to know."

Zbirak stood up. His eyes were hard. "Let me make one thing clear." He slipped the icepick from his pocket and held it up for her to see. "I'm the only one who will make demands here."

And then he drove the icepick into Bob's chest.

39

CASSIE SCREAMED WHEN BOB DID. THE SHADOWS CLOSED IN, AND SHE thought she was going to pass out. Her awareness landed on the fear of Zbirak turning to her next. Writhing against her ropes, she managed to slip her whole right hand free.

"Please," she begged, struggling to keep focused on escaping while checking on Bob. "Please don't hurt him."

"Oh, it's a little too late for that." Zbirak let go of the icepick, keeping it lodged in the man's chest. "As long as I don't remove it from his chest, he won't bleed out. He'll be in tremendous pain." He laughed like the very thought brought him joy. "But he'll last longer."

Cassie was sobbing now, barely able to focus on freeing her other hand.

"I'll make you a deal." He stepped back from Bob, his hands in the air. "If you answer my questions truthfully, I'll give you a sixty-second head start. It's been a long time since I had a proper hunt, and something tells me you'll make for interesting prey."

Cassie gulped in air, unable to keep from staring at the instrument stuck in Bob's chest. He had stopped screaming, only because he'd passed out from shock. She looked back up at her captor. "What do you want to know?"

Zbirak pondered the question. Then he took a step closer and leaned down, until they were face to face. "What makes you so special?"

"I don't—" She cut herself off and cleared her throat. She had to be smart and give him what he wanted. Anything to prolong the inevitable. She scratched at the ropes around her other wrist, but they were so tight. "I'm not sure why Apex is so interested in me. I didn't even know they existed until earlier this year."

"Ah, yes. Your trip to Charlotte." He stood up straight and began pacing the room. "Your file goes back farther than that. To the night you were almost killed by Mr. Novak. Did you know that?"

She shook her head. Words had escaped her. A shadow had formed over Zbirak's shoulder. At first, she thought it was his—cast by the overhead light. But no. It moved separately from him, drawing close, then backing away. Then it turned toward Cassie. She thought it might've locked its gaze on hers, but it didn't have eyes.

A chill went down her spine.

"Ms. Quinn?" Zbirak took a threatening step toward Bob.

She had to think about what he'd just said. "N-No. I didn't know that. I've never seen my file. I don't know what's in there."

"It says you're a psychic. Is that true?"

"Yes."

"Prove it."

Cassie had a hard time ignoring the shadow. It moved closer again, giving Zbirak a wide berth. "What?"

"Prove it. To me." He swept his arms out to the side. "Make me a believer."

"It's not that simple."

Zbirak gave no warning. He stepped over to Bob, and twisted the handle of the icepick, driving it deeper into his chest. The other man screamed, and Cassie rocked back and forth, nearly toppling the chair over in the process. Their captor waited until they were both quiet again. "Make it that simple."

Cassie took a deep breath and closed her eyes, feeling the other presence in the room. It was weaker than most other spirits she'd encountered before. It felt far away.

Zbirak took a step closer. "I'm losing my patience."

"Someone is here. A spirit. They've been following me all around the city. Trying to reach out to me, but I don't know why."

"You'll have to give a more convincing performance than that, Ms. Quinn."

Cassie ignored him. The shadow drew closer, as though hesitant to finally make contact. It was weak, but it had waited so long for this. As the tendrils of its shade slid across her skin, a searing heat scorched her from the inside out. Full of pain and frustration and the kind of anger that never goes away. Growing and growing until she didn't think she could take any more. Sweat beaded across her forehead. She might've cried out, but she couldn't hear anything aside from the burning inferno roaring in her ears.

When Cassie was certain she was about to pass out, the heat faded. It was slow, and her skin prickled like she'd been in the sun too long, but it was calmer now. Gentler. Like a warm summer day. Unbidden, she thought of California, of the golden coast. The sea spray on her face, and the smell of salt in the air. A happier time. A time before the pain.

As the feeling faded, she was left with the dregs of someone else's memories. Thoughts and feelings and experiences that weren't her own. And even before opening her eyes, she could feel she was alone with the two other men. The shadow had dissipated. Gone forever.

"California." Her voice was hoarse, parched dry from the imaginary heat.

Zbirak waited a beat before he spoke. "What did you say?"

Cassie opened her eyes, half expecting to still be in the sun, next to the ocean. "She was from California."

"Who was?"

"I don't know her name." Cassie licked her lips. They felt cracked and burned. "She loved the ocean. Did you know that?"

"Who are you talking about?"

"The woman you helped bury. The one Reed killed. She wasn't

even dead when you set fire to her body. She felt it, every excruciating second, until her mind couldn't take anymore. When she finally gave up, she thought she'd go somewhere nice. Somewhere cool. But she never left. Not when she had unfinished business."

"How did you know that?" Zbirak's voice was hushed now. He didn't sound afraid, but harbored an edge of danger. Like an animal who knew its hunters were closing in. "How did you know about California? Did Reed tell you that?"

"No. She did." Cassie looked up into Zbirak's eyes, and for the first time, she felt no fear. "Did you know spirits draw power from the energy left behind when they die? That's why you only see them lingering in certain spheres of influences. Where they died. Where they're buried. But sometimes they're drawn to the people who had an impact on them—like their loved ones. Or the ones who killed them."

"I've killed a lot of people, Ms. Quinn." Zbirak was starting to recover. "What makes this one different?"

"That's what I'd like to know. Sometimes it's who they were. Sometimes it's how they died." Cassie licked her lips again. She was returning to normal, too. Her other hand was so close to slipping free. "She's dead and buried in California, but her spirit was here in Chicago. That's a long way to travel, and she wasn't even haunting you. She was following me. That's why I could only see a shadow. She spent so much of her energy trying to contact me, she became a shade of herself. She was too far from her place of unrest to go back. She had to make her final contact count. And she did."

"Reed could've told you any of this. I'm still not convinced."

"You prayed over her grave. She thought it was a strange thing for an assassin to do." Cassie let her words sink in. "Reed had left, crawling back into whatever hole he'd come from. But you stayed. You prayed over her. Something tells me you don't do that with everyone you kill. Why her?"

"How did you—"

"I told you, Mr. Zbirak. I'm psychic. Do you believe me yet?"

Zbirak's smile was rotten from the inside. "What else did she tell you?"

"That she's seen enough of the other side to know where you're going." Cassie's other hand slipped free. Now she just had to bide her time. "And you should've been more afraid of dying while you were still alive."

Zbirak studied Cassie, and she wondered if he believed a word she'd said. There were still scattered thoughts and memories buzzing inside of her like a hive of bees, but whenever she tried to capture one, it would slip free. Who knew when they would settle and reveal more of the puzzle?

And who knew if she'd be alive long enough to put it together?

Cassie flinched when Zbirak moved, but he had merely taken a step back. Then gestured toward the stairs and the door that led to the first floor. "You held up your end of the bargain, Ms. Quinn. You may go."

Cassie froze. "What?"

"I'm sorry to say your element of surprise is gone. I noticed you slipped your bonds about a minute ago. My fault for not tying them tighter." He held up a finger. "However, you were honest with me. You're a truly fascinating person, Ms. Quinn. I hate to see you die. But you've left me no choice. Luckily for you, I've decided to keep my promise. I told you I'd give you a sixty-second head start. The clock starts now. If I were you, I'd start running."

Cassie didn't hesitate. Throwing off the ropes circling her torso, she took off up the stairs without looking back. If she could get Zbirak away from Bob, perhaps the other man would survive the ordeal. But that was only if she could outsmart an assassin.

The seconds ticked by like bullets firing from a gun.

Time was not on her side.

40

CASSIE HALF EXPECTED THE DOOR AT THE TOP OF THE STAIRS TO BE locked when she reached it. Wouldn't it be like him to offer her a chance at survival, only for her to find out it hadn't been real all along? But Zbirak had kept his word, much to her surprise, and when she wrapped her hand around the cool metal doorknob, it twisted easily under her touch.

After pushing through the door, she slammed it behind her, hoping to give herself a few extra seconds. Pausing long enough to glance around the kitchen, she looked for a butcher knife, finding nothing she could use to her advantage. It was clear Zbirak hadn't been living here.

As she took off through the living room, she wondered if Zbirak would leave Bob alone while he was counting down the seconds. The man's only hope of survival was if the assassin found Cassie a more interesting prey. Besides, he still needed Bob if he intended to get to Rose. Bait was bait, even if it was a little worse for wear.

Cassie unlocked the front door and burst outside, pumping her arms in rhythm with her legs as she launched herself off the front steps. She raced into the woods, knowing it wouldn't give her much coverage. Even though the trees were thick, they were bare.

Plus, there was the little fact that he knew these woods better than she did. She had no idea where the road was and which direction they had come from. Were there other houses around here? Would anyone be willing to help her? Even if she made it somewhere safe, Zbirak would be able to follow her footsteps in the snow.

This head start was nothing but false hope. Zbirak had dangled her freedom in front of her face like a carrot on a stick, only so he could watch the light leave her eyes as he snatched it away.

She needed a new plan.

Ignoring the instinct to run, Cassie tucked herself behind a tree and closed her eyes, slowing her breath. Reaching out with whatever sixth sense she had, probing the woods, she searched for an escape route. The trees had an energy to them, like they had seen Zbirak pull this trick too many times before. But the spirits were shy. They were in hiding. Still scared of him, even in death.

Cassie had lost track of the time in her head, but it was closing in on sixty seconds. The trunk she leaned against felt safe, but not for long. After pushing off it, she kept straight, jogging but not expending all her energy just yet.

There was a subtle shift around her, some feeling that tugged her to the left, back behind the house. Letting it pull her, she trusted whatever part of the universe had guided her this far. Maybe it was delusional—the desire to believe someone or something else was looking out for her—but she was willing to take that chance. It hadn't steered her wrong yet.

A branch snapped behind her, and Cassie sped up. A tingle crept its way up her spine and wrapped around her neck, sitting there like ice-cold fingers against her skin. Zbirak was behind her, but he hadn't pinpointed her yet. He was still on the hunt.

She still had a chance.

Cassie pushed harder, trying her best to stay quiet. Now she could see the back of the house. The yard was bare of any ornamentation, and she kept to the trees to stay out of sight. Part of her wanted to go back into the house, to trick Zbirak into thinking she'd escaped, only to lock the doors behind her and use the house as a defensible point. At least she'd be able to keep an eye on Bob.

But it wasn't meant to be. She'd taken her eyes off the path in front of her for a few seconds to check her surroundings, and when she looked back, Zbirak was standing there, dead ahead, a gun in one hand and a smile on his face.

"You should've been quieter, little mouse. I could hear you from across the yard."

Cassie swallowed back the bile that had risen in her throat. The feeling that had drawn her in this direction tugged harder, forcing her to circle around until Zbirak's back was to the house. "You're not going to get away with this." It was the only thing she could think to say. "I have friends who will search for me. They'll never stop until they find you."

"I've heard that before." Zbirak raised the gun. "Any last words?"

Cassie had been in this situation before—defenseless, staring Death in the face. She'd had her life flash before her eyes plenty of times before. But this time was different. This time, she felt like she was in the right place at the right time. "Do you have any regrets?"

Zbirak must not have expected the question because he hesitated, tilting his head ever so slightly to one side. "Come again?"

"Do you regret anything you did?" Cassie stood firm now, legs rooted to the ground. The cold seeped into her boots, but she didn't move. She felt like she was waiting for something. A signal, perhaps. She'd know it when she saw it. "Killing people, I mean. Have you ever had regrets?"

"No." Zbirak frowned. "Not until today. Not until you."

"Me?" Cassie hadn't expected that answer. "Why?"

"You're different. Special. It seems a waste."

"You don't have to, you know. You can choose."

"Oh, I know." Zbirak was still frowning. "I am choosing. Choosing to live with this regret. I truly am sorry, Ms. Quinn. If it's any consolation, I feel as though you'll find solace on the other side."

Cassie opened her mouth to say something, anything, to get him to extend the moment even a few seconds longer. She didn't want to die, and as many times as she'd imagined how it would happen, she never thought it'd look like this.

Zbirak took a deep breath, holding the gun steady.

His finger twitched toward the trigger.

There was a loud bang, and Cassie jumped, waiting to feel the impact of the bullet.

But there was no pain. No fear. Zbirak's mouth dropped open at the same time blood blossomed from the side of his head. His eyes went dark, and his body crumpled to the ground. The gun fell from his fingers, unused.

Cassie looked around wildly, spotting a figure running toward her through the trees. It took her a few seconds to put it all together. The dark hair in a high ponytail. The long coat snagging on branches along the way. The black gun gripped between her hands.

"Adelaide?"

"Cassie." The detective was breathless. Slowing as she got near, she kicked Zbirak's gun away from his hand and then bent down to check his pulse. He must've been dead because she tucked her own weapon away and grabbed Cassie by the shoulders. "Are you okay? Are you hurt?"

"I'm not hurt." Cassie hadn't realized how afraid she'd really been. Tears poured down her face. "I'm okay."

Harris pulled her into a hug that stole her breath, lasting a full minute. Harris wiped sweat from her brow with the sleeve of her jacket. "What were you doing out here? Why didn't you run as soon as you saw him?"

"I knew." Cassie swallowed, trying to get her thoughts in order. "I knew if I just stayed there, it would be okay."

Harris shook her head. "Someone's really looking out for you, I guess."

Cassie looked back toward the house, her stomach dropping as she remembered Zbirak's other victim. "Bob! He's injured."

Cassie took off toward the house with Harris right behind her, calling after her to stop and let her go first. Cassie ignored her, bursting through the front door and charging down the stairs. She heard Harris curse behind her, but their attention was stolen by the man in the center of the room.

The ice pick was still lodged in Bob's chest, and though his rattling breath was certainly cause for concern, the weapon had kept him from bleeding out—at least for the time being.

Harris knelt next to him, checking his wounds. "He doesn't look good," she said. "We need to get him to the hospital."

Cassie wasn't about to argue. It took a few minutes, but they stripped the ropes from his chest, and together, they hauled him up the stairs. His head lolled back as they dragged him out the door, and Cassie had to fight back tears. After all that, she couldn't imagine him dying. Not now that Zbirak was gone, and the danger was over.

Harris must've read her thoughts, because after gently laying him across the back seat of the rental, she got behind the wheel and took off toward the nearest hospital. Cassie stayed in the back, watching Bob fight for his life.

41

By the time they reached the hospital, Bob was unresponsive. His face pale and gray, and though he was still breathing, Cassie had noticed his heart rate slow dramatically as the rattling in his chest got more distressing.

Harris made it to the nearest hospital in record time, pulling to a screeching halt in front of the doors to the emergency room. Several nurses rushed outside with a gurney when they saw the two women pulling him from the car. Harris tucked a pair of Polaroids into his shirt pocket before he was whisked off to surgery, and they stuck around long enough to give one of the staff his name and information about what had happened to him. Once their backs were turned, the detective pulled Cassie back into the car and took off before anyone could stop them.

Cassie twisted around in her seat, waiting to see if anyone noticed what they were doing. "Shouldn't we stay?"

"You positive you're not injured?" Harris asked, taking her eyes off the road long enough to give her a once-over. "You need to tell me if you are."

"I'll have some nasty bruises," Cassie said, touching a gentle finger to her face, "but I'm fine."

Harris looked down at the clock on the dashboard. "We don't have much time."

"For what?" Cassie turned back around and settled into her seat, putting her seatbelt on just in time for Harris to whip out into traffic. "What's going on?"

"After I noticed you were gone, I had to wait until the cops showed up to take away Thompson."

"The janitor?"

Harris nodded. Looking over at Cassie, her eyes were full of regret. "I'm so sorry. I should've come sooner. I just didn't want him to escape. I—"

"It's fine." Cassie put a reassuring hand on Harris's arm, and she felt the other woman relax beneath it. "Really. I knew you would show up. I wasn't worried."

"That's a lie." Harris barked out a laugh. "But I appreciate it, anyway." Turning back to the road, she switched lanes and flipped someone off when they beeped in protest. "Someone had already called the police, so it didn't take them long to show up. But I had a few minutes alone with Thompson."

"What did he say?"

"Tried to cut a deal with me. Said Reed wasn't paying him enough to take the blame for everything. Told me if I let him go, he'd tell me everything I needed to know about Reed."

Cassie put a hand to her mouth. "Did you?"

Harris shot her a look that said, *you know me better than that.* "Told him I didn't trust him. Needed to know what he had before I considered it. He said Reed was playing both sides, and once Aguilar found out, he was a dead man."

"Playing both sides? How?"

"Don't know. As soon as the cops showed up, I handed his ass over. Snuck off before they could get ahold of me. They'll probably figure out who I am. Security footage and all that. But I'm not worried about it. We'll be out of here before they catch up to us."

"Where are we going?"

Harris smirked. "The airport, of course."

Cassie groaned, hoping Harris wasn't suggesting they add another leg to their trip. "Why?"

Harris switched lanes, taking an exit at the last second and pinning Cassie to the door as she leaned into the turn. "Reed is running. We got too close to him. Thompson said he was headed to the airport. So, that's where we're going."

"What, O'Hare? We're never going to find him there."

Harris didn't take her eyes off the road. "We have to try. We're so close to something, I know it."

Cassie looked down at her hands in her lap. "You know how we saw the name Zephyr in the spreadsheet?"

"Yeah."

"That was Zbirak." Cassie felt like she had a rock in her throat. She couldn't swallow around it. "He killed David."

Harris stiffened but didn't look over at her. After a moment, she whispered, "You're sure?"

"He said it himself. I don't think he was lying."

Harris swallowed, and Cassie wondered if she was having the same trouble as she was. "That's good to know. We should, uh, call someone to go check out the body. If he really was a hitman, they might be able to close a lot of cases now that he's dead."

"Maybe we should just forget Reed," Cassie suggested. "Go home, take this one day at a time."

Harris shook her head. "Zbirak might've pulled the trigger, but someone hired him. We have to prove it's Aguilar. Then we can rest. Then we can try to move on."

Cassie wasn't so sure. Learning that David's killer was dead should've been a relief to Harris, but Cassie could tell she was more determined than ever to push forward. Even if they got to Reed, and eventually to Aguilar, what would it change? David would still be dead, and Harris would still carry the guilt of his death on her conscience, warranted or not.

"I think Reed might be heading to California."

Harris finally looked at her, and Cassie didn't miss the tears that had pooled in her eyes. "What makes you think that?"

Cassie relayed what happened in the basement with the shadow person. Still unable to construct all the images the spirit had tried to pass on, her gut was saying they were on the right track. "If Reed's running, he's trying to make sure no one uncovers the skeletons in his closet. He'll go there first. I can't tell you why, I just—"

"You just know it's true?" Harris smirked, but it didn't reach her eyes. "Yeah, you say that a lot. I've stopped questioning it."

"Really?"

"Out loud, anyway."

Less than ten minutes later, they pulled into the long-term parking at O'Hare International airport, and Cassie jogged to keep up with Harris after exiting the car. By the time they made it to the ticket counter, Cassie was out of breath. She pretended to go through her duffel while she returned her heart rate to normal. Harris had told her they weren't going to get on a plane tonight, but the detective had insisted they bring their bags, just in case.

Harris slapped her ID and credit card down on the counter. "We need to get on the next flight to L.A."

The woman behind the desk didn't look alarmed. She tapped away on her computer, asked Harris a couple questions, took their IDs, and swiped the credit card. A few minutes later, they had their tickets in hand and headed toward the security gate.

"What about your gun?" Cassie whispered before they approached the guards.

"Left it in the car," Harris said. "We'll need to get Jason's guys to hold onto it for me. And return the rental." She grimaced. "I'm not risking any late fees. They're ridiculous."

On the other side of security, they stopped in front of the departure screens. There were five flights heading to L.A. within the next hour. Harris pointed to the two leaving from Concourse B. "You look for Reed at those two gates." She pointed to the three leaving from Concourse C. "I'll look at these three. Let's meet back here in an hour."

"And what if we spot him? We can't hold him against his will."

"Whoever finds him first calls the other one. Then we make a scene."

"Make a scene?" Cassie's throat constricted. "And do what?"

"Say you saw him acting weird. They'll hold him until they figure it out. We'll call the cops. Explain what's been going on. It'll be enough for them to look into what he's been up to."

"And what we've been up to."

"That's a risk we'll have to take." She pulled out her cell. "I'll call in Zbirak's body. There'll be enough physical evidence to back up your side of the story. Especially when Bob pulls through."

Cassie didn't know what else to say, so she nodded her head, shouldered her bag, and headed toward Concourse B. She'd flown through O'Hare a couple of times over the years, and despite its size, the airport was easy to navigate. What wasn't easy was looking for a needle in a haystack.

And that's exactly what Reed was.

It only took a few minutes to get to the first gate, which had just started boarding. Unless Reed had gotten on first, he wasn't here. Cassie hung around for a few minutes to make sure he didn't show up late.

It took another couple of minutes to walk the length of the concourse to get to her second gate. Every few seconds, Cassie checked her phone to see if Harris had called. It had been frustratingly silent. Did that mean she hadn't found him, or was she too busy causing a scene?

The crowd thinned as she approached the second gate. There was just a single person waiting to scan their ticket at the desk. The woman behind the counter had bright orange hair and a bored look on her face. The man standing in front of her was short and fat.

Cassie recognized him instantly.

"Hey!" A few heads turned, but the woman with the orange hair didn't pay any attention to her. Reed gathered his ticket and shuffled through the door. Cassie called out again. "Hey!"

Reed looked over his shoulder, and then did a double take. When he recognized her, a huge smile lit up his greasy face. He raised a middle finger in her direction before turning around and running down the jetway. The woman with the orange hair shut the door after him, cutting Cassie off from her target.

"Hey, I need to get on this plane." Cassie reached for the door handle, but the woman stood in her way. "Please, it's important."

"Doors are closed."

"Please, I—"

"I'm sorry, ma'am, but the doors are closed. There's nothing I can do."

"That man you just let on. Donald Reed? He shouldn't be on that plane."

The woman looked Cassie up and down. It hadn't occurred to her what she must've looked like. Were the bruises Zbirak had given her already blossoming on her face? "He had a ticket." She moved away from the door to close up her station. "Do you have a ticket?"

"Not for this flight, but—"

"Then you don't belong on this flight. Have a good day."

Cassie cursed and walked over to the window, watching as the doors closed and the plane got ready to taxi to the runway. He was so close, yet so far away. She called Harris, who picked up on the first ring.

"Any luck?" the detective asked.

"Just missed him." Cassie looked over at the screen above the counter. "He's headed to L.A."

"You didn't try to stop him?"

Cassie tried to keep the annoyance out of her voice but didn't succeed. "I tried. They wouldn't let me through. He was already on the plane. They closed the doors."

Harris sighed into the phone. There was nothing they could do now, short of calling in a bomb threat. And that wouldn't end well for either of them. "Let's meet at our gate. Hope you brought another change of clothes."

Cassie hung up with an exasperated sigh of her own.

Next stop: Los Angeles.

Cassie Quinn returns in *Betrayed in Shadow*! Pre-order your copy now: https://www.amazon.com/dp/B09S6TJGBJ

Join the LT Ryan reader family & receive a free copy of the Cassie Quinn story, *Through the Veil*. Click the link below to get started: https://ltryan.com/cassie-quinn-newsletter-signup-1

THE CASSIE QUINN SERIES

Path of Bones

Whisper of Bones

Symphony of Bones

Etched in Shadow

Concealed in Shadow

Betrayed in Shadow

ALSO BY L.T. RYAN

Click on a series name or title for more information

The Jack Noble Series

The Recruit (free)

The First Deception (Prequel 1)

Noble Beginnings

A Deadly Distance

Ripple Effect (Bear Logan)

Thin Line

Noble Intentions

When Dead in Greece

Noble Retribution

Noble Betrayal

Never Go Home

Beyond Betrayal (Clarissa Abbot)

Noble Judgment

Never Cry Mercy

Deadline

End Game

Noble Ultimatum

Noble Legend (2022)

Bear Logan Series

Ripple Effect

Blowback

Take Down

Deep State

Rachel Hatch Series

Drift

Downburst

Fever Burn

Smoke Signal

Firewalk

Whitewater

Aftershock

Whirlwind

Tsunami (2022)

Mitch Tanner Series

The Depth of Darkness

Into The Darkness

Deliver Us From Darkness

Book 4 (2022)

Cassie Quinn Series

Path of Bones

Whisper of Bones

Symphony of Bones

Etched in Shadow

Concealed in Shadow (2022)

Blake Brier Series

Unmasked

Unleashed

Uncharted

Drawpoint

Contrail

Book 6 (2022)

Affliction Z Series

Affliction Z: Patient Zero

Affliction Z: Abandoned Hope

Affliction Z: Descended in Blood

Affliction Z : Fractured Part 1

Affliction Z: Fractured Part 2 (Fall 2021)

ABOUT THE AUTHOR

L.T. Ryan is a *USA Today* and international bestselling author. The new age of publishing offered L.T. the opportunity to blend his passions for creating, marketing, and technology to reach audiences with his popular Jack Noble series.

Living in central Virginia with his wife, the youngest of his three daughters, and their three dogs, L.T. enjoys staring out his window at the trees and mountains while he should be writing, as well as reading, hiking, running, and playing with gadgets. See what he's up to at http://ltryan.com.

Social Medial Links:

- Facebook (L.T. Ryan): https://www.facebook.com/LTRyanAuthor

- Facebook (Jack Noble Page): https://www.facebook.com/JackNobleBooks/

- Twitter: https://twitter.com/LTRyanWrites

- Goodreads: http://www.goodreads.com/author/show/6151659.L_T_Ryan

Printed in Great Britain
by Amazon

84050986R00133